NEW TREE
TWO STORIES

by

NATHANIEL
SCHELLHASE
HVIZDOS

Product of the United States of America
Third Printing 2020, All Rights Reserved
Greenback Books (ain't no thing)
natetwostars@gmail.com
Social Media Presence: @natetwostars & Nate Two Stars

ISBN - 9781709878558

Dedicated to Ted

My Haunted Friend

May He Find Peace Before His Death

Special Thanks

to

Ruth

-

Daughter

Sister

Mother

Aunt

Grandmother

INTRODUCTORY INTEROGATION

Do you want your granddaughter to grow up showing great promise only to die in a gutter under a bridge alone with a needle in her arm from a heroin overdose? Paint this image in your mind over and over again knowing the only answer is a definite "No!"

Unfortunately, our children are dying at an astonishing rate nationwide in constantly evolving variations of this theme. The horrible fact is that young people and old people are experiencing hardships today across the United States where stress and poor role models lead to hard drug addiction which hooks them into a downward spiral without even realizing it is happening. Why?

The information provided by the medical industry and others entrusted by society with guidance for wellness and health for the public are falsely leading people into a dark hole of poverty of spirit generated by doublespeak and substance abuse. Since my youth the message disseminated to me and the people of the United States has been "Say No to Drugs" and a "War on Drugs" has been declared. This literally translates into a policy of "do not" buy drugs on the street and a concerted effort to wage a war on common citizens.

It tears me apart to know that if you buy amphetamines or opioids from a neighbor then you are a criminal who can be sent to prison for this criminal behavior. This is the "War on Drugs" that enforces a hard line against drug addicts, drug use, and illicit drug sales. Organized crime and violence surround this entire process where guns, large amounts of money, and gangsterism are glorified through popular media and publicly condemned by formal society at the same time.

The justice system is overwhelmed with revolving doors of human beings corralled into bad situations without any true rehabilitation efforts being supported by government policies. Reentry services for returning citizens are minimal and underfunded nationwide, where only a few benefit, and false information is given to unprepared individuals when they are released from incarceration. Factually, justice is now a business where privatized prisons and jails are expanding nationwide with private entities making profits generated from the incarceration of drug offenders, our neighbors and our family members who are all essentially people caught in a sad situation. Think about that please.

Juxtapose your mind now to the formally accepted drug afflicted class of people who are the other end of this spectrum. Remember "Just Say No." How about "Just Say Yes." Do you say this is crazy to even suggest that taking hard drugs is a good thing and that they should be in wide use by people on a regular basis? I say addiction to opioids, amphetamines, and other dangerous manmade substances should not be acceptable and are not good for people due to their long-term detrimental effects on health and overall wellness. That is my clear truth. Truth. You do not want your granddaughter or your grandson to die in a gutter under a bridge alone with a needle in their arm from an overdose.

Now please let me knock on your door. For example, suppose you get injured or have a mental health diagnosis, which many of us do. Do you know someone close to you in physical or mental pain? When this happens, our families, friends, and individuals reach out to professionals for assistance. We ask for help from professionals who are in positions in our culture, who are deemed experts by our established leaders, to remedy and solve our health problems. And these professionals advocate for and prescribe medicines that can potentially kill you, addict you, and ruin your lives and those of your fellow neighbors.

The drugs prescribed for ailments will in themselves cause new and often worse long-term life altering ailments. Now we have a "Say

Yes to Drugs" society where prescriptions are handed out, with no care for the pain and suffering that are handed out with them. And so here we are in a quandary. Welcome to America. Wake up and do something to solve this problem. Make a decision to help each other and do justice for your fellow neighbors. Show the world that we are a great people and we are a great country. Sing loud that we are free and intelligent.

Vincent Thunder Star

COP
DOCTOR
DEALER

Cop Doctor Dealer

Dick

I write in wax on plastic underwater. I am the policeman and television trancing with that ringing noisc. And you lose stuff. I am crazy, but other people lose stuff too. Brain washed and ingrained with blah, myself and others. There is always the next millennium.

I do not drink alcohol until after midnight. Reading "variation is lower than background noise" just as the tape player stops its music. All too common a phenomenon, this synchronicity. This grace.

I started stealing as a youngster, emulating the gangster persona. Just like the World Trade Organization, having allies is important and most important of my allies was Schmerrer. At the ripe age of thirteen we formed the Irish Mafia of Richmond. Schmerrer was our leader. He was the strongest. Others in the mafia were Hoss, Ferret, Ananda, and Xean [pronounced Shawn]. While we were all in it together, Schmerrer, Hoss, and I were the closest. We started robbing houses together in seventh grade. It was not every day. In fact, it was not even every week. We went through binges. Five houses in our first week.

Oh how our adrenaline rushed! We looked for alcohol, money, and sporting goods. Most prized were skateboards, usually taken from houses of people we knew. Richmond was our venue. The unsuspecting. We would knock on the door and if there was no answer we would find a way to get in. It was on.

But that is not when I started stealing. Oh no. I was much younger when I started. Striking out however possible against the other. That included just about everyone.

My Plan

I chose to be a cop, a great career. At twenty two I had been working in retail for six years. Then my cousin became a police officer and so the idea hit me. By twenty-four I was a full-fledged police officer with an Associate Degree in criminology. Now I could do whatever I wanted and no kid was safe because I knew all the angles of suburban youth.

Perhaps I would set up my own arm of the law, sort of permissive and beneficial to me.

Perks

It is my first day on the beat in my own cruiser, number forty eighty. In the trunk I have a shotgun, for what I do not know, and software giving me satellite positioning through my computer. I carry a nine millimeter semi-automatic pistol on my left hip with hand cuffs and stun gun around the back as well as an extra clip of bullets. On my right hip I carry a night-stick and a blackjack thumper. I do not wear the optional hat or tie. My hair is groomed to a flat top which I get cut every week. I work three twelve hour shifts per week. Work is work, but my work is full of perks.

Free food from the coffee joint managers, not that that is a big deal. I do not get tickets from other officers for anything. Three months went by quick. Ladies really dig my uniform. My patrol includes the evening sports events at the local high school. Females give me the eye all the time.

The Game

"Have you ever shot anyone?" she asked with big ocean swimming batting eyes and a wide smile.

"Only with my camera," I said.

"Hah, hah! You're so cute," she said looking up at me with her killer aqua spheres. This could be the end, but it is not.

"So when are you done here?" I asked.

"I have to cheer until the end of the game," she paused and continued, "then I could use a ride home."

"Well I have to stick around until the crowd thins, until maybe ten thirty," I told her.

"That would be good," she said.

"Alright. I've got my eye on you."

"I was hoping you did," she flirted and giggled. Then she joined the other cheerleaders. Though I was crowd control, I kept my eyes on her tight young curvy body all night, hardly able to control my own excitement with no one to talk to about it. What I wanted was illegal and could cost me everything. So what!

There were two other officers at the football game. I was posted at the home team bleachers. Fred was posted on the opposing side's bleachers and Jim was posted at the entrance gate. I do not even know her name, but at halftime she sure looked good.

We had spoken at other games, but never before arranged for me to drive her home. I wonder how old she was. To protect and serve I could say in my defense of a young lady without transportation, another lie. I bet she is at least sixteen. Who cares? No matter what, I want some of that. I definitely cannot be seen with her in my car.

As is my job, I paced back and forth along the front of the bleachers until the final tick of the clock. The home team won by two points, fourteen to twelve. The visitors needed a better kicker. They were from the west end. Back in high school, we used to smoke in the bathrooms and outside in this stadium between classes and before school. After school it was up to the shopping center where we bummed change and smoked and spit. What a time! I haven't smoked since I was nineteen. It has been that long since I hung out at the shopping center.

Soon it would be just me and her in my car. Did I mention, she has dark brown straight long hair to the middle of her back? Oh ho! I love long hair. So what if she was young. Many cultures marry their ladies at such young ages.

"Ready?" she asked with a smile and her head tilted to the right.

"Let me pick you up at the end of the parking lot," I said.

"Okay," she bubbled.

"I hope I won't regret this," I informed her.

"You won't," she assured me. Within few minutes, the crowd dispersed for the most part and I was out of there. I got in my car, turned my driving lights on, and slowly rolled to the back of the parking lot where there were not many lights. There she was. Young. Sensuous. Oh ho! Ambrosial sunshine.

"Hi," she said.

"Hop in."

"I've never been in a police car before," she revealed.

"That's a good thing. Whadda ya think?"

"It's interesting. You got a computer right here."

"Yep."

"It smells new."

"We keep our cars pretty clean." There was a pause of silence, then I continued, "So where do you live?"

"I was thinking of something a bit more intimate," she said.

"Intimate huh?" I questioned.

"Yeah, like the Comfort Motel."

"Ha hmmm."

"You think that's funny?" she asked.

"It's just that you're so forward."

"That's how I like ta be." She tried to move the computer. It did not budge. "I wish we could move this thing out of the way."

"I can't really take you to a hotel."

"Oh, I see!" she gruffly said.

"No, I want to, but I have to work another six hours before I get off."

"I'll get you off sooner than that." She reached over and went for my zipper. Then she made me a law violating policeman. Yeah, knowingly getting sexual with a high school girl. "Do you have a handkerchief or some napkins?"

"Check the glove compartment," I told her.

"Alright." While I drove, she found a napkin with her right hand. She excited me dangerously. She wiped me up and zipped me away. My mind was blown!

"How about a hotel next time?" she asked.

"Sure," I said. She navigated me to her house and then kissed me ferociously.

"Bye."

"Bye." She got out and headed to her door. I left without even making sure she got inside safely.

The Shipment

"Hey Schmerrer."

"What's up Dick?"

"This and that," I said.

"Cool."

"Did you get the shipment?" I asked.

"Straight from good ole China," replied Schmerrer.

"I can stop by to pick it up later."

"Well," Schmerrer said, "I got a date at seven."

"So I'll be by at six thirty."

"Solid."

"Alright, peace."

"Late," Schmerrer said as he hung up the phone. It was our way of saying 'Later'. Schmerrer is an apothecary. He gets domestic drugs, but most importantly he gets shipments from other countries which we turn around through our connections.

Hoss is a sort of local kingpin for pills in his network. I guess D.C. too. We clear about three hundred grand a year split three ways tax free. It keeps us in all the finest restaurants and gold jewelry. I expect one day I will have kids and maybe I will clean up then. Either way, I have a lot of cash for now.

My Attitude

What I hate most about being the fuzz are drive-alongs. You know, where a citizen rides along with you on your shift. I have to be polite and nice the whole time, like I am some Miss Manners. I have only done it twice and let me tell you, they were the longest days ever. I have a mom and a dad and two living grandparents and that is enough nicety for me. Always 'Please' and 'Thank you'. Yes sir. No ma'am. I am too tough for all that. Shit, I can bench three ten.

If you ask me, and you are, I could care less about pleasantries. I get to bust people, mostly for traffic violations, and then they pay the government which in turn keeps my paychecks rolling in. You are damn right I like authority. Do you know what really feels great? Putting people in hand cuffs. That practically gives me an erection. That and young women. Their total helplessness almost makes me laugh every time. I like taking corners a little fast when I have someone in the back. Nine out of ten, they topple over. I really enjoy putting the cuffs on too tight so the offender bruises. Then there is the thrill of pushing them into the car so the guy hits his head on the door frame. Ooops.

And I hate when some scum tries to make friends with me. Someone who feels it necessary to chatter.

"I'm not here to be your friend," I tell them point blank. Then if that does not work, I tell them, "Shut up!" When we get to the station, they know it is business as usual. No comradery with the violator, just go by the book and try to stick as much to them as possible. If they get out of line, I have no qualms about twisting someone's arm behind their back. I have done that a number of times.

As an officer of the law I have the right to squash insurrection, any sort of it. Non-compliance with my commands means it is their mistake and they get forced to the ground into submission. The lawyers sometimes see it as excessive, but what do they know? They are just a bunch of book worms, stuck behind words in the safety of the courts and offices. They are lucky if they ever have to throw a punch in their adult lives. The most violence they take part in is eating a cheeseburger. The only crimes they witness are on television or in a movie. They are not on the streets dealing with psychos.

Every day I deal with the potential of being killed because of my work. That is why we carry guns, to protect ourselves in dangerous situations. When I am out enforcing the law, chaos is always a possibility. There is mayhem abundant in our society and it is my job to defuse it.

Sure. Most people look normal, but what are they thinking? I say it is the normal people we have to worry about because they are able to disguise their unruly thoughts and behavior. At least when we see some freak with long hair or blue hair, we are warned that they have their own values and to take caution when dealing with them.

I have been told that the best police never draw their guns, but I say that is bullshit! When I see a driver reach under his seat, my gun is drawn and on them until I have ascertained what the suspect is retrieving. I do not think I can be too careful. There are crazies and all I need is an excuse.

In The Mix

Knock, knock, knock. Ding dong. A moment later the door opened.

"You're busted," I said. We both laughed, Schmerrer and I. "What's up Schmerrer!"

"What's happenin' Dick!"

"Coolin'."

"Alright, alright. Come on in."

"Sure," I said as I entered.

"How's everything?" Schmerrer asked me.

"Good. So who's this date you got lined up and does she have a friend for me?"

"She's an accountant and I wouldn't even ask her if she had a friend for you."

"Why not? You think she'd be afraid of me? I am a veritable monster of muscle."

"You are quite a monster. Ha! No, I don't want anything to come between us, at least not until I check out her drawers."

"Gotcha," I said.

"Cool?"

"Yeah man." Into the kitchen we went for a glass of water. Got out a glass. Filled it. I sat down at the kitchen table, a glass square table. High backed slatted wood chairs. Schmerrer followed in with a box. He put it on the table.

"Ruffies. Valium. Oxy. Addy. Ecstasy. Xanax. Tranqs," he reported the contents.

"Yeah man, I am headed over to Hoss' house directly."

"Good deal bro."

"So, you gonna let me stick around and check out your hot date?"

"I don't think so." I chugged the rest of my water.

"I'm out," I said.

"Late."

"Peace."

Hoss

I am Hoss. My house is a suburban mansion to an inner-city person. Four bedrooms and two full baths upstairs. Two attics, one above the two car garage and one up in the eaves. On the ground floor I have a large entertainment room, a kitchen with a cooking island, an eating nook, a dining room, and a television room. Off of the television room is a spacious screened in porch. In the basement I have two large carpeted rooms, one with a pool table and the other with ping pong. Then there is a small room with a fold out couch and a full bathroom. Also in the basement is a dark room for photography.

I am neck deep in this business with Dick and Schmerrer. What they do not know is I have more profit than I let on. They have been out of the scene for a few years so they do not know the value of our business. I have a landscaping business which pays my rent, but get most of my money from the pills. I do not take them myself, well not often anyhow. Maybe once every few months. My woman and I take some and hang out at home together. We are not crazy like the punks, hip hops, ravers, hippies, and such who enjoy using psychoactives in public. I guess the adrenaline rushes I get from dealing keeps me naturally drugged enough. With every deal there is always the potential of getting busted. I keep a shotgun around just in case. If I go down it will not be without a fight, but Dick keeps that probability to a minimum. He is in on most of the busts which are far and few between. Far and few.

It is my job to keep our products flowing to our distributors. I do a damn good job. If things slow down, I have to find more distributors. I clear two hundred thousand a year for myself and a little over a hundred thousand each for Schmerrer and Dick.

All I do is smoke weed, take and make calls, and eat, as well as commit acts of sexual bliss with my girl. I am fat. Three-eighty-five and six foot nine. My hands are as big as basketballs. My balls are as big as Hawaiian waves in the Winter.

Family

My mom and our friend Charlie exchange milk chocolate balls every year at Christmas. The hilarious thing is they use the same balls year in and year out. Charlie is a freaky long haired ex-NAVY forty something taxi driver. If my mom did not marry my dad, she could have gone for Charlie. Charlie is not married, but has had the same girlfriend for as long as I can remember. He has his military background and so he knows how to kill people. He has been trained for such. He always seems nice, but there is something about him that says to me he is sketchy. I think he loves all of us. I hope that never changes.

Psyches

As you can see, the characters are all blended with a single reference to mom and dad. There is no differentiation as to who they belong. Therefore there is a breakdown of psyche barriers. One must re-establish the psyche barriers. Re-establish the barriers and work towards communication to break down barriers. A myriad of choices, but something that must be done. I will thus identify these parents referenced as Hoss' lineage.

And know this. In the future all people will have personal gardens. If you will, I am the omniscient presence. I may interrupt from page to page for clarifying remarks. Ado.

Schmerrer

So this customer comes in and demands a refill on her Ritalin. This lady was another kind of breed. She was grotesque in physique and weighed four hundred and twenty five pounds with breasts the size of watermelons. She left a trail of stench that could be smelled at a distance. I am Schmerrer, the apothecary. I am the pharmacist who gets the drugs. When she came to the counter, the pharmacy clerks were not prepared for what was about to go through.

The lady dropped off her prescription with fury in her eyes. Her hands were wet from perspiration and her eyes were flaming from the absence of her Ritalin pills. The first words out of her mouth were, "GOD damn it, can I get some fuckin' service over here for GOD'S sake?" She was terrible, the worst customer ever. The clerk had to approach this one with caution. His first impression was that of a giant slug. The woman seemed to slide across the floor as if slowly pursuing the scent of beer. I was bewildered from behind the counter. I had never seen her before. I did not care if I ever saw her again.

Officer Sibe

Jen Sibe was on the case. She hears guitars when she plays drums and she tries to give money to bums. She believes in magic, but she believes it to be evil. Ten hut!

Shop Talk

Two of Dick's fellow cops talking.

"It's a lie that the kids are all okay."

"We've really got to do something soon."

"I heard one young person say they were so scared to quit smoking pot."

"Quite interesting. That person will probably never amount to anything."

"Fuck work."

"Yeah, let's go get coffee."

"I bet Perry Farrell loved a girl named Jane."

"Or some son of a bitch in their band did."

"So why are you still fuckin' here anyway?"

"I don't know."

"I thought you said you were either moving into the city or out to the country."

"I did say that, but life here is so sweet, and it's where I grew up."

"Fuck yeah!"

"I know, I know."

"So what's up with that friend of yours from the ARMY who's a lawyer?"

"Yeah, always getting thugs off the hook."

"Yeah."

"Marquez."

"Yeah, Marquez."

"Fuck Marquez!"

"Yeah right." Police officers are so classy when they socially interact among themselves. At least these guys were honest.

Dick

I was just working twenty four hours straight without sleep on a special assignment doing the good work I do.

I just lay around dreaming all the time. Pig guts on my karma. I had coffee for breakfast and lunch which is reaped through child labor in some Latin American country. I am dreaming awake and the aliens are on their way. I need sleep, but the captain says we are here at least another two hours.

"I've been told that I am too bold," I said to Officer Lucy. "You're at your peak you know," I continued.

"If you believe I can read your mind," Lucy replied, "you may be scared from what I find." It hit me.

"The boss was ripped off at Twenty-Fifth and Broad," said the lead investigative officer. Lucy and I continued to talk in the back of the room.

"Now I'm an asshole," I said. "Can you tell what I'm thinking now?" Lucy got a grin.

"Don't say it." Soon enough the meeting was over and I had a new phone number, that of my fellow Officer Lucy.

It was next Friday and I gave that teenage girl a ride home again. No hotel yet, but again there were sexual favors during the ride. All because I am a cop and I enforce the law.

Jen's Lead

"And that's all?" Jen asked.

"Yes ma'am."

"Thank you for your time. I believe you are now free to go about your business. If there is no objection. Ladies? Gentlemen?" the Judge said.

"No."

"No. Ah."

"Nope."

"Good day," Jen said and the smiling suspect left, released on his own recognizance. Jen was onto to something. The case would fly after all.

Mexico

Mexico in a laboratory.

Two shakes of dexellyponisaph. I have completed the formula! He addressed his assistant. Take this prescription and do not call me. I will be in the lab and cannot be disturbed. I remain unperturbed in the face of investigation. There is no relation of myself to the suspects in the case. There is no trail to follow. No trial to go to. They think they can trace it back to my office door. The capsules I make are too pure to be caught. My skills are bought and sold at a high price, higher than what I paid for my education. My successful career is crooked pharmacology. If three pills were blues and four pills whites, four thousand dollars makes it alright.

With law and unlaw committed to crime, all that is required of me is time and willingness to be. And I will still be anonymous in the end which is near. My instincts sharpened for fear tell me to be safe, careful. When a punch is thrown, I duck.

Taste Of Fear

"What do you mean, why am I paranoid?" asked Schmerrer. He went on, "Why aren't you paranoid is the question? There is a war going on against us if you hadn't noticed. We are wanted men as soon as all cards are shown."

"Frankly, I'm quite bored with this discussion," said Dickie. "As long as we stay smart, all is okay. No worries. Comprende amigo?"

"Tell 'im what you told me," said Hoss.

"What?" asked Dickie.

"About the bombs," Hoss relayed.

"Oh yeah," recalled Dickie. "I'm more worried about nuclear war. There are so many bombs with a bunch of needle heads in charge. That's how I think we're all gonna go." As you can tell, Dickie is a bit strange with atomic weapons. Why worry about them? Later in their conversation, Hoss revealed a slice of how he does what he does.

"I work on the mind," he said, "talking to people with my right eye focused, my left eye focused, or with both eyes focused on them. I try to play into their soap operas and can do it for a while. Then situations seem so condemned. I feel bad that I am happy the way things are for me," Hoss stated.

At The Game Again

Zap! The victim was tazzered. He fell to the ground. And then he went unconscious. Why? He was drunk at the football game where Dick's beat happened to be. The assailants did not wish to rob him. They just wanted to get him, the other.

"That'll take care of that asshole. Boom! Hah! They'll never suspect us straight edgers to have done this," called out the one in the group who actually held the weapon. Straight edge means no intoxicants of any kind. Some straight edge folk smoke cigarettes or drink caffeine, yet still refer to themselves as straight edge. This is an example of variation within a category. The exception to the rule. The group thought they were unstoppable and out of the public eye, but no.

"Which one of you punks did this?" asked Dick. He was patrolling the outer edges of the arena when he happened onto the situation.

"Oh shit!" They all ran. Dick did not chase. He immediately went to the victim's aid.

"Knock knock," said Dick into his radio.

"Who's there?" came the voice of the dispatcher.

"This is Dick over at the game. I need an ambulance. There is an unconscious person here. ASAP!"

"Ten four. ASAP!"

Dick The Liar

They say you cannot trust a lair, but I know I can be trusted and I am basically a liar. I mean every day I swear an oath to uphold the law and yet every day I am breaking the law in carrying out my business with Hoss and Schmerrer, among other things. At least they can trust me is what I am saying. I do not think I would risk my life for other officers.

They are all such stick in the butts. Truly, why would I risk my life for theirs? They all believe in a corrupt system. I see the faults in society and have formed my own methods for coping. These other police officers think they are making a difference by handing out traffic tickets day after day. They really need to get a grip on what is what. Do they honestly believe that giving out traffic tickets, enforcing driving laws, keeps an orderly society? They probably do believe that. Me? No. I see how it is, capitalism. Supply and demand.

Truth in capitalism is that all should be allowed to do what they want as long as they are not disturbing the well being of others. And so you can see why I am in business with Schmerrer and Hoss, capitalism.

If all drugs were legal, the world would be a much freer place. As it is, criminals no different than your average business person run the streets with people like me running interference with the rest of law enforcement. I am not the only one doing it. It is a system full of double talk, thinking one thing and doing the other, but I do not let on.

“Captain,” I said, “when are we going to do some raids? I’m amped to do some real work.”

“In time. We’ve got a few investigations under way. We’re still collecting evidence right now,” said the Police Captain.

"If I can help now, in any way, I'd like to," I said.

"Well, how about some information processing?"

"Yeah, sounds good."

"Can you come in on Friday?"

"Certainly sir." And so I had done it. More extra work, but it will let me in a smidgen closer to the action and believe me, I need all the angles I can get. This takes me one step closer to knowing who the narcs are, something a man in my position needs to know. These wouldn't be my first secret assignments and I'll probably get in on some busts.

Yeah, big busts. Bullet proof armor and weapons drawn. I don't mind busting people. I find it exciting. I am not scared of being killed or injured. You have to be tough, take a lot, and also be lucky from time to time. I've had a bullet hit me in the chest. My vest saved my life. The bullet could have easily hit me in the neck, hands or feet which are not safe zones. My captain has talked to me about becoming CIA, FBI, or ATF someday. He tells me to get a few years experience in law enforcement before moving to the national or the international level. I say okay, he knows best.

So I go out on another routine night, pulling over speeders and other traffic law violators. Cops were jerks when I was sixteen. There were real criminals, like murderers and such, who they could be out arresting instead of giving me a ticket for not having a proper sticker on my license plates. Now it is me out busting people for petty offenses. I can see other people thinking I am lame and so I understand there is a cycle. My goal is to be as cool as possible.

Cuisine For Hoss

I forgot to write this chapter. How about introspection and culinary insight.

"You see," commented Hoss, "cold weather people are short mannered because of all the time spent with only family inside their shelters during Winter. I don't mean recently either. I mean from generations dating back through evolution." As you can see with this revelation, Hoss is very introspective. How about a new perspective?

Cook sliced rings of onion in olive oil and add lengthwise sliced asparagus to the mix. Add tofu, broccoli, and spicy peanut sauce. Also add a thinly sliced skinned apple. Sauté. After a few minutes, throw in some mushrooms and a glass of red wine. Serve on rice.

That is how Hoss gets it.

Schmerrer Workin' It

My main goal is to get the drugs out there. They sell themselves. People seek out pills. I just have to stay apprised of all new people in our niche. I am real good with names and faces, as well as asses and chests and tattoos and credit cards.

The thing with a trick is this, if she is nice then talk with her and if she is not then joke with her to try to elicit acknowledgement of being. Get information.

Out at the punk show…

"Hi."

"Hi."

"I'm Hoss."

"Oh." Bad. She did not introduce herself. Keep going.

"What's your name?"

"Olivia."

"Olivia, I've been seeing you around." She furrowed her brow. "Were you at the 'Assholes' show?"

"No," she replied.

"No?"

"Wait, yeah I was." She rolled her eyes and the edges of her lips curled slowly up.

"Oh yeah? Were you at the Super Bowl of Hardcore?"

"Yeah."

"See, we're into the same shit." Oops. I try not to cuss during initial contacts.

"Did you see 'Melt Banana'?" she asked.

"Yeah."

"They're bad!" as in totally awesome.

"So what do you think of this band?"

"They're alright." She was turning away to look at the band. What more could I do? There was no click occurring so I grabbed her ass. She squinted and lost her smile, pointing at me with her left hand which held a cigarette. "Hey!" she blurted.

"What?" I asked trying my best to sound innocent. Then she smiled again.

"What's wrong with one fucking?" she asked leaving me speechless. This was a joke of some sort that didn't really seem to make sense. I guess 'one fucking' is masturbation.

"What?" I stammered.

"It should be two fucking." She made me laugh, 'two fucking' means sex. Really though it wasn't too humorous. Olivia vividly smiled and then laughter. And that was a no-brainer. The dig was in. Somehow, even with the raucous music we were able to talk.

"Where are you from?" I asked.

"Wheaton. How 'bout you?"

"South, near Richmond."

"Richmond?" she echoed.

"Yeah. You know where 'at is?"

"Yeah, I've been there."

"Yeah," I said, "it's alright. Is Wheaton cool?"

"Yeah, we got 'Phantasmagoria'."

"Yeah, that's right. It's the record store where bands play. I was at an Avail show there a couple weeks back"

"Me too," she said.

"I think I mighta seen you there."

"My hair was pink then. Now it's black," she informed me. Duh, I could see it was black.

"Chicks with pink hair are rad."

"Thanks," Olivia grinned. I guess it was a compliment somehow even though her hair was then black.

"You wanna go somewhere where we can kiss?" I proposed.

"Okay," she said to my surprise.

"Really?"

"Psyche!" She got one on me.

"Ooof! That's harsh!"

"Could I maybe get your phone number?" I asked.

"No."

"Why not?"

"You're lucky I didn't hit you for grabbing my ass."

"I thought chicks dug that kind of shit." Damn, cursed again. No wonder she will not give me her digits.

"Not me."

"Sorry."

“Yeah, and we also don’t like being called chicks.”

“What should I call you?” Time for me to learn something.

“Ladies.”

“Ladies?”

“Yes, ladies.” I felt it was time to retreat. I had a chick at home so I was not really pressed about hooking up, though I do like the excitement of variety.

I ambled to the bar and asked for a water. I had to drive that night out of D.C. and did not want to risk it by drinking.

Jen And Missy

AAZ 127.

TBS 640.

Missy Plunk was on the case in conjunction with Jen Sibe. This night they were taking license plate numbers at the local store that sells rolling papers. Boring cop shit that is supposed to be exciting. Then it bubbled a bit. They were in the mountains where they could snowboard when they were not working, though they actually worked all day, every waking moment.

"Here's a strange one," said Jen. Into the parking lot pulled this car, a Chevy pick-up truck, with a couple of surf boards in the back. Their Texas tags read 'SLICK'. Now that it was in the street lighted parking space, one could view painted fire adorning the front of the ride.

"We've got to follow this one," continued Jen as she perked her attention, folding up the paper upon which they were recording information. Into the store they went and sure enough their suspect was buying rolling papers and no tobacco. That means the papers are for drugs.

Trailing The Suspect

They got in their car and followed 'SLICK' to his house.

"I wonder if zombies know how to drive," said Missy to Jen. They had the movie Dawn of the Dead on their caravision system.

"I don't know, but I'm talkin' about takin' this guy like goin' to a mall during a sale. Serious shit, ya know!" said Jen.

"Yeah," Missy concurred.

"We're gonna get this suspect."

"Have you seen those different dollar coins?" asked Missy.

"No."

"They got Sacajawea on 'em."

"I've got your Sacajawea right here."

Mohawk

For cover, Jen needed a haircut. She was going to get her hair cut like a horse. It was to Lake Anne Cuts for the primo do. The wash. Hair back with a sensually friendly young lady.

"Hi. I'm Lilliputian," said the hair washer.

"Jen Sibe," she said as she extended her left hand in greeting. Jen sat herself in the washing chair, slightly reclined with her neck comfortable on the curved plastic basin rim. She closed her eyes and tried not to engage Lilliputian. However, that was not achievable.

"I hope you tip me and tip me well," said Lilliputian. "I'm married and we're trying to buy a house. We figure buy a house and in a couple years I'll start popping' 'em out." Jen caught the break in her words. She opened her eyes to address the youngster.

"Children," Jen enunciated carefully, "are a big responsibility." The hair washer fell silent and washed. Naje slipped her a five upon completion. Another five to write off on the tax payers. Then she was in the haircutting chair. A man was to cut her hair, her choice.

"Hi, I'm Kenny. What can I do for you today?" Naje looked calm.

"I want a Mohawk," she said.

Making A Connect

"Guitar picks with grips," said Kenny. "That's my million dollar idea." Jen was looking in the mirror, trying to decide if she liked the Mohawk. Kenny was about done. He asked, "So whatta ya think?" Jen had to force something out.

"Radical," she said.

"Yeah, radical." Kenny was diggin' on Jen and he questioned, "So, you goin' to 'Piss Test' tomorrow?"

"I don't know." Then she asked, "Where's it at?"

"At the Balcony."

"Where's that?"

"Between 9th and 8th on Royal street."

"What time?"

"They're headlining so they probably won't be going on until midnight at least."

"I might go," Jen replied.

"It'd be cool to see you there," he said. Naje smiled. He asked, "Bang, bang. What's your name?" Naje had a prepared answer.

"Denene."

"Alright Denene. Hope to see you there."

Winner

They were back on the trail of 'SLICK' of whom they now knew the registration name on the tags, Race Kinder. It was night and the culprit did not even close his blinds. With a long telephoto lens, Naje and Missy got pictures of the assailant rolling joints on the kitchen table.

"Home base," said Naje into her radio.

"Yeah."

"We've got a winner. Can we give 'em the prize?"

"Give 'em the prize," said the voice from home base.

"Out."

"Late." Another sweepstakes winner. Naje and Missy got out of their car and marched to the front door. They knocked.

"Police! Open up!" they commanded.

"Just a minute," called the voice from inside. Then it was all over.

Suddenly there was a boom and the door had a hole in it. Missy lost her abdomen. She was ripped in half. Naje was to the side and received none of the shotgun blast. She dove off to the right and hit the ground. She aimed her gun at the door in case the guy tried to come out that way. She saw Missy pass into death.

Everything slowed down. Naje's brain was working extra fast. A blue pick-up truck took off down the driveway from the car port. The license plate was covered in mud. Someone would have to pay!

Overview

Omniscient vision.

Naje Sibe may never get involved with our characters.

Amateurs

Hoss and his bro, Josh, took the evening to go skateboarding. Very dangerous are these little rolling objects. Four wheels that like to spin fast. Joyful foot powered vehicles.

Some professionals take these bad boys down large hills at speeds upwards of fifty miles per hour. Others take them onto massive structures called half pipes which can launch them five or ten feet into the air where they perform a cornucopia of tricks. Hoss and Josh were very much amateurs. Their quest on this evening was to ride down parking garage levels at mellow speeds. Calm relaxed cruising.

It is a shame that skateboarding is illegal in many places with signs posted forbidding the activity. Josh and Hoss knew the spots where there were no signs. They were free to ride, a feeling only a skateboarder knows.

Hoss had been skating since the seventh grade, age twelve. When he was younger he used to ride ramps and skate parks, his favorite being Vans at Potomac Mills which is a little over an hour from his home. Back in the day, administrators made it a rule that no skateboards could be brought to school. Even then Hoss broke the rules by bringing his board to school. You can see a pattern to the criminal mind.

Traffic Death

Pelting hail descended. It was most fitting. Richard was on patrol when he got a call to report to an accident. He responded immediately. Upon arrival he saw it.

A van had hydroplaned into oncoming traffic and smashed head-on into a tractor trailer. The remains of the two people in the van were in pieces mixed among crumpled metal and shattered glass. Blood spattered among the debris. It looked horrible, like something out of a war.

The hail ceased, returning back to rain. There was work to be done. Body parts had to be collected and sorted. Blood had to be checked for foreign substances. To remove the legs they had to cut through mangled metal. Though there was death, its fetid smell was not yet present.

This was Richard's first death on duty and he found it repugnant and fascinating at the same time. How people are one minute air breathing souls and the next, nothing, Richard contemplated. He would have to write a report. How would it start? How would it end?

Gnarly. Gruesome. Sickening.

All these words came to mind as descriptors, but none really explained it. None could capture the emotion he felt. He had seen people in movies vomit from seeing such things, yet he felt no nausea. If he smoked, he thought, now would be the time to smoke.

Instead he stood around with a few other officers and talked while the emergency crew took care of business. Business. Minutes leap-frogged minutely.

"It's a shame," one officer said.

“Fate,” another said. Looks like human coleslaw, Richard thought but did not say.

Instead he said, “It’s too bad.” Then the chief officer on the scene spoke.

“We’ve got their IDs. Someone is going to have to tell their families. Any volunteers?” There was silence and raised eyebrows.

“Richard, you’re new to this,” said the captain, “aren’t you?”

“Yeah,” Richard admitted.

“Then how ‘bout you take care of it.” Could he deny the chain of command? He did not want to do it, but he had no choice

“Should I wait until after the autopsy?” he asked.

“You can wait until this evening, but it needs to be done today. Here are their IDs. Copy down their addresses and give ‘em back to evidence when you’re done.”

“Yes sir.”

“Oh, and one more thing.”

“Yeah?”

“Shave that shit off your face.”

“Captain, the officer’s dress code permits…” Richard got cut off.

“I don’t care what the code says! It looks bad with the uniform. Okay?”

“Yeah.” What an asshole, Richard thought, but again he kept it to himself. He knew there was a time to shut up and now was that time. He once heard that the less you speak the more you learn and so he was trying to learn at this point. He wrote down the deceased’s digs and gave the IDs to the detectives. Everyone on the scene walked as if in a stupor. No one wanted to rush things. It was such a grim situation. They were there to save lives which were impossible in this case. Here they were just to clean up the mess. The bloody gory mess, a task so serious, so sobering. Then there were the other commuters wishing they could get home without any respect for the dead.

Groceries

'4 20 03'

'09 May 03'

Hoss and Josh were now at the store checking expiration dates. These were clearly past expired.

"This store sucks," Hoss said with a laugh.

"Yeah right," said Josh. "Maybe we can get this stuff for free."

"Why would we want it?"

"Free food man."

"Yeah, but it isn't good anymore."

"Man, I'm low on cash and I'm willing to risk it," revealed Josh.

"Why didn't you say something," Hoss said. "I'll buy you some groceries."

"For real?"

"Of course bro."

"Verdad?"

"If I have then you have-just ask,"

Dilemma

GOD, I am sorry for thinking you lived behind the mirror, thought Richard. In his spiritual delirium of late, Richard had become fascinated by mirrors and actually believed he could communicate with GOD through them.

"Please let this go well," thought Richard out loud to the company of the Latino counselor riding in his car.

"Yeah," said the counselor, "and hopefully we are with GOD." Richard found it odd she said that just after he was thinking of the ALMIGHTY. They were driving to one of the dead men's homes.

Dead man number one.

Richard knocked on the door.

"Did you know the discovery channel was bought by the military?" the counselor asked him before the door opened.

"What?"

"Yeah," she said. The door opened long.

Babies

"A baby!" exclaimed Hoss.

"That's right," assured his girl.

"When? How? I mean how long until…"

"Seven months to go," she informed Hoss.

"Jesus! I'm gonna be a dad! I have to make some calls!"

"Can I first get a hug?"

"Oh yeah! Anything you want mama!"

Soulmates

"If GOD is all-knowing and we are all part of GOD, then are we not all-knowing? I mean seriously, ya know," Schmerrer said to his date Alexis.

"Well Schmerrer," she paused to find the words, "if A is B and B is C, then classical education tells us that A is C, but I don't think that we are all-knowing like GOD." Schmerrer took it further.

"Like could a dog be a soul mate or even a fly?"

"I don't know baby. Oh look, P and 14th. We're almost there."

Dealer

I am Schmerrer the apothecary. I supply people with drugs for a living. An amazing world with these narcotic cocktails. I am so wasted. Some people cannot afford expensive prescriptions while others pay only one dollar for the same thing. The companies seem to be in business of profit rather than healthcare.

I want another cigarette.

<u>Armor</u>

"Attack! Attack!" they were commanded as Richard and his three compatriots entered the practice room where the dummies reside.

"Cover me!" shouted one as she entered the doorway. A gunman's image popped up from behind a couch.

Bang! Bang! went her gun. Two to the chest, good aim. One down. Would there be more? A forced entry into a criminal's house can get ugly. Luckily police have body armor to protect them.

Trail Mix

Naje Sibe is on the case. Hot on the trail of someone, though who, she is not quite sure. Was it this Race Kinder? Naje heard through an informant that a big deal was coming through Dulles Airport on the fifth of May, only two days away. She had a new partner by the name of Saul Biggs. Saul was older than her by seven years. He had a polished attitude, straight and narrow, and polished mirror sunglasses. He wore a suit every day.

Together they fought the forces of evil. Saul saw criminals as the scourge of the earth. He was ready to kill each and every lowlife so his children could live in a world of only good people. Saul was an idealist, so he thought. Perhaps he judged too much which is not his job. Judging should be left to juries and judges.

There was supposed to be a shipment of credit cards coming through on Air Power Airways, flight 123 arriving at 7:20 PM. Supposedly the shipment would be carried by a woman by the name of Reda Petcoe. She was to be met by none other than Joe Bosconi, a felon who had served prison time for grand theft auto twice. So now he had changed his racquet, but his angle was still against the law.

They knew what Bosconi looked like and would have him marked the entire time. Overweight, peach skin and black combed back hair, usually wearing tinted glasses and in casual dress. That was Bosconi. The task force, of which Sibe was the key player, consisted of airport security, ten plain clothes officers, and Naje and Saul. Bosconi's photo had been circulated and studied by all the participants. They would definitely know his whereabouts the whole time, but what of this Reda? She was the wild card, unknown until the time of the transaction.

Cinco de Mayo.

The airport was its regular bustle. Luggage. Metal detectors and bomb personnel. Departures and arrivals. Baggage claims and all the workers. The baggage claim area for flight 642 was under surveillance by some twenty law enforcement officers.

And there he is, Joe Bosconi, wearing his glasses with khaki pants and a black and pink bowling shirt.

"Bosconi's in play," Naje said over her radio.

"Check," came back Saul's voice. "I see the duck." It was ten minutes until the on-time flight. Joe stood alone, calm and collected. Everything seemed to be going as planned. The police team was all around Joe. In seats. By a rental car counter. By the bathroom. Two by the exit and two dressed as airport baggage men, set to help with retrieval and such. They were ready for Reda Petcoe, whoever she was. Joe was not getting out of this one. There was nowhere for him to run.

The plane arrived. Upon the passengers arrival to the baggage area, Joe stood waiting and erect. In minutes Joe was embracing an elderly woman. The officers approached as they got her bags.

"Joe Bosconi," Naje said, "you are hereby under arrest."

"What about it?" Joe asked.

"Reda Petcoe I assume," continued Naje.

"No," said the elderly woman, "I'm Aretha Bosconi."

"Nice try. You are both under arrest." Naje then proceeded with formalities and had them both handcuffed.

Hours later their admitted identification checked out. It was Joe's mother and there were no fake credit cards. And Naje's informant was now found out by the criminals he attempted to inform upon.

The End

And everyone lived happily ever after.

Recap

Don't go Disney on me!

Girrrls

"Hey man, ya wanna go to the movies tonight?"

"I'd rather watch something on cable. I got fifteen movie channels and over a hundred regular channels."

"Yeah, but don't you get bored?" asked Richard.

"Not with Jessica coming over."

"Really?"

"And with Maureen coming over."

"Oh, I see. Sold out over a couple chicks."

"You got it," replied Hoss.

"Well I gotta work for the next two nights," asserted Richard, "so how about we hang out like Saturday or Sunday?"

"Cool."

"Alright, I'll hit you later."

"Late." They hung up their phones.

Unlike Hoss and Richard, who put in a regular work schedule, Schmerrer works sixty to seventy hours a week. He is really dedicated to pill pushing, after all, he is a sanctioned drug dealer. Sure, the drugs he sells have been tested for safety. That's good, but is he not just another dealer? Why not sell pills to the underground? And you know what, he makes more off his pills than he lets Hoss or Richard know. Like Hoss, he is scamming his partners.

Everyone has to look out for themselves. Schmerrer pulls in thirty thousand more than he lets on. Quite a nice chunk of change.

He saves a lot in order to fulfill his dream of buying a sailboat and retiring early to live a life on the ocean's broad horizon. Oh yeah! Tropical island living with no fixed address. Posh lifestyle, right on it, with fish a bounty for daily meals.

But right now, now, he is lost in the sea of criminality, illegality, crooked smuggling. The easy life with only one possible outcome. Pure adrenalin racing through the hours, waiting for the badge with the handcuffs knocking at his existence.

Undertow

"I gotta get out."

"Well there's the door," replied Richard with a motion towards the exit from the room.

"No, I mean all this."

"Whatta ya mean, 'all this'?" asked Hoss. The three were all hanging out at Hoss' on Saturday night.

"This illegal activity," professed Schmerrer.

"What's wrong Schmerrer?"

"What's wrong? I'll tell you what's wrong! I wake up at night freaked out by the sounds my house makes, afraid that it is the cops coming to bust me."

"But Schmerrer," entered Richard, "I've got all that covered. Man, I'm in on all that. We are safe."

"Yeah Schmerrer," added Hoss. "It's cool."

Broken Rules

"Bouganvia's the name," said the tall wiry African American man as he extended his hand across his desk to Naje Sibe.

"Nice to meet you," she said. She knew he was a special assignment officer.

"As well for me." He paused then added, "I'm not going to chase my tail around. We are re-assigning you. Naje nodded and said, "Okay."

That breaks the boundary of two people speaking within the same paragraph. And Naje was never seen again.

Deceased

"I'm already dead."

"Come on Schmerrer."

"Well I'll tell ya one thing!" togged Schmerrer.

"What's that?" asked Hoss. Schmerrer's face went blank.

"I forget." Then he took another bong hit.

Stuntman

The headlines of the Washington Poster read, ‘Falsified Elections Here in America’.

“Let’s face it,” Hoss said, “this whole country is a sham! What about the Indigenous Native Americans?”

“Come on Hoss,” Dickie said, “we’re not responsible for that.”

“Right,” Hoss said as he chuckled. They did not talk for a few minutes as they watched a television show about police. Then Dickie spoke.

“When I was like twelve, we had this pick-up truck and my dad would drive fast like ten miles an hour, and I’d run next to it with the door open already. Then I would jump in stuntman style.”

“Yeah?” Hoss had to get verification to make sure Dick was not pulling his leg.

“Yeah.”

“That’s some cool shit.”

<u>FMX</u>

The night was glaring with moonlight on the snow covered landscape. Schmerrer sat in his living room watching a moto-cross trick show digital video recording. The riders were fearless. They jump thirty feet into the air and do back flips with their motorcycles. Or thcy makc a jump and land with their feet holding the handlebars. It was insanity, practically. He was enjoying himself on this Sunday evening.

Church today had been interesting. The priest actually asked for GOD'S blessing of our nation's fighting troops. Schmerrer thought he should be asking for an end to violence rather than blessing our troops.

Kids Kids Kids

"What we need is a strong cabaret of services devoted to the involvement of youth and elderly citizens," says Dickie.

"Yeah, this country's a show," expudiated Hoss. He meant it with very strong conviction.

"I'm not sayin' that!" retorted Dickie. "All I'm sayin' is there's a lack of national effort to accommodate kids and retired persons." Then Hoss went seemingly off track.

"Well all I'm sayin' is everyone is lookin' out for themselves and theirs. Like look at the deodorant industry."

"The deodorant industry?" queried Dickie.

"Yeah. You don't need deodorant. For one it causes man-boobs. All you need is daily showering for hygiene and you know, deodorant is marketed to teens on up." Hoss was convinced he was making sense. Dickie got back. Hoss eventually came to this point... "Well jail keepers should be strip searched in and out of work." Dickie gave a sour glare. Hoss reiterated, "Yeah nude searches!"

"Well... that makes sense, I guess, really," admitted Dickie. Hoss was impressed with Dickie's honesty. "And I'll tell you this," Dickie said wide eyed, "they shouldn't be allowed to have their own individual garments. All of them should have to dress without individuality." Hoss thought they did that already, but did not interrupt.

"They should all have the same haircuts, a monthly crew cut and no facial hair. Women too," said Richard the officer. Hoss liked Dickie's enthusiasm.

"Yeah!" approved Hoss. "Right on!"

Faith

"Ramadan starts Friday," said Schmerrer. It was part of Schmerrer's obligation to celebrate the holidays of Islam. Just like a Catholic celebrates Christmas even though they may not be very religious and have doubts about a man born of a virgin and returning back alive after being crucified to death.

Schmerrer was not a very good Muslim. He drank, though not alcoholically, and he did other mind altering substances too. Mushrooms. LSD. Grass. He did not really see why they were illegal except for the timeless adage, 'Divide and Conquer'. Still he fasted and visited with his siblings and parents. Even his grandma was still alive. She lived medicated and without family present and in an assisted care living facility.

Quite a mouthful to get all that out. At the end of the night Schmerrer lays down for sleep and prays, just like most other American folks. He guessed his GOD ALLAH was the same GOD as the Christians' and the Jews'. For the polytheistic angle, his opinion was a bit muddled. He just did not think about it was all.

Bus Drivers

"I can tell you this," Hoss said with exasperation, "bus drivers should make at least sixty big bones a year instead of their hiring part time wage at ten eighty an hour."

"Big bones?" Dickie ebleted.

"Thousands," Hoss dryly related.

"It must be tough," Dickie decreed.

"What?" asked Hoss.

"Carrying the weight of the world on your shoulders."

"Why do you say that?"

"You always have social conscience when you speak Hoss."

"Just worry about yourself Dickie, and everything will be okay."

Nil

Saul Biggs had a man inside the rave scene. Pills for them were a mainstay. Ketamine. Ecstasy. Oxy. Addy. Anything in between. Hoss sold directly to the 'X Squad' who worked the clubs.

Saul Biggs was close, but did not know it. He has made so many promises to clean up the world from human poisoning drug dealers. And so far he had accomplished nil. That was going to change.

Toni

The television was on. The talk show host eloquated, "All I can quote about this comes from a favorite writer who said, 'Change, not exchange'. That's from Toni Morrison. She is a novelic poet, master of the written tongue." Schmerrer clicked off the teevee, though the words made sense. He had to get something to eat and stop dilly dallying. He skipped his evening work-out because he was sore from inline skating the night before.

As he ate his dinner, he reminisced about the days of youth when he was straight and alert. Straight edge, but not violent like some of today's straight edge gangs. Then he fell in with the fellas and he began to experiment. He remembered wanting to pursue righteousness that only children know and could barely grasp these memories. It was a time when only love was known. Now look what he had become. Lost.

Bank Accounts

The User. He amazes himself.

"Look at it! Look at it," Jesus told his boys. He held out his Mickey Mouse wallet in each of their faces. "Look! Look!" They all looked at it. "My cousin Lucky gave it to me. It's bad! She smokes a lot of grass. Y'all would like her." Jesus smoked much doobage and loved his cousins who did too. His friends smoked too and also did a lot of pharmaceuticals. Hoss and his partners depended on people like Jesus and his friends.

"Guess what I did yesterday?" Jesus asked his crew. They had no idea.

"Que?"

"I got a check in the mail from my grandma and wanted to cash it at the bank from which it was written, but only the drive thru was open. The drive thru is for account holders only, so I made about five calls eventually speaking to a vice president of the bank. She said just this once I would be allowed to cash my check at the drive thru even though I did not have an account there. You wanna know what was funny?"

"Yeah. What?"

"The drive thru is only for cars and all I have is my bike, ya know, so I got her to let me drive thru on two wheels." His friends smiled. "Pass that shit…" Jesus was very impressed with his own resourcefulness. His friends thought his action with the bank was great. His friend Carlos told him so.

"That's so cool man. You should run for office with that politicking shit."

"They would never take me. Hey let's call Hoss. I have a hundred bucks."

"Right on!"

Power

“Work is nothing like school,” Hoss told Jesus. Hoss was checking the college radio station. Fuzz. Then he got it.

“Who? EMI!” sang Johnny Rotten of the Sex Pistols. He let it play.

He was driving into D.C. with Jesus and a box full of pills. Hoss felt unlimited in every way. He kept the speed limit.

“You know,” Hoss told Jesus, “we don’t really have any power in this country. It’s all the military who control us. The police are just sanctioned thugs representing the property owners.” Jesus did not say anything, so Hoss continued, “Except for people like you and me who work around the law.”

“Yeah, I hate pigs. Fuckin’ classist bastages!” Jesus’ veins popped out on his neck when he said this, obviously riled up.

“That’s right. Trying to keep the poor working at all costs, but why do we make eight bucks an hour while others make hundreds an hour. See, ‘Protect and Serve’ is applied to merchants and the rich.” Hoss moved into the fast lane and went on, “The only way for a truly free society is to abolish weapons, such as guns and bombs.” Jesus listened as he tapped out a beat on the dashboard. “Look at mentally ill people. I got a sister who’s on psychoactive medication which makes her sleep all the time. She collects disability and you know how much she gets a year?”

“How much?” asked Jesus.

“Eight grand a year. That is poverty mi amigo and that is in the richest country in the world. Now that mi amigo is pitiful. It’s like the country just gives up on you and sweeps you onto the garbage heap.”

“Yeah dude. I’m with you.”

Library

Sitting around the house is Schmerrer's favorite thing to do. On this Friday, no work, so he does just that. Most likely he would involve himself in evening television. He has no date this night. During the day, as he sat in front of the teevee, he read, drew, and wrote. Then off with the teevee and on with a little radio to calm his spirit. His more favorite thing to do is this.

"Alright man, I'm goin' to the library," Schmerrer said into the phone.

"Have a book of a time," Hoss razzed him from the other end of the line. "Get booked up," he joked. Schmerrer hung up the phone, put on his sandals and he was in his car.

A sixty nine Ford Mustang and driving that Mustang was really his favorite thing to do. Drive! On nice days he would put the top down and turn the music up. He had a hundred CD player in the trunk with a remote and full internet connectivity. He had a fantastic assortment of music. Then off to the library.

Whatever

"All government jobs should be year round, not this short year shit that Congress works." Hoss was serious.

"Whatever bro," Dickie said fluffly.

"Yeah right, whatever. That's the problem in this country. Everyone keeps saying 'whatever'."

Set Ups

"It's all a set-up!" Schmerrer declared.

"What?" asked Hoss.

"Half of what goes on."

"What?" Hoss reiterated.

"They're out there, I hear them." Schmerrer's eyes got big as he said this, "They're scratching the walls."

"Look man, there's no one out there," Hoss said confidently. "You want me to go look?"

Schmerrer did not reply. Hoss continued, "I am going to look." Hoss went outside. Schmerrer's paranoia was getting worse. He thought about going to jail more and more.

Hush

Hoss pulled a big toke from his bong. Dickie watched, but did not smoke. He got tested and had given up ganja years ago. Hoss did not know how he could do it.

"You wanna hear my theory on computers?" Hoss probed.

"Shoot," replied Dickie with the less you say the better off you are attitude.

"Well, you know how we send signals into outer space trying to communicate with other intelligent life?"

"Yeah."

"Well micro technology has arisen through contact with tiny microscopic life forms. Let's be for real, no one could design computers by themselves. All those on and off, zeros and ones code. No, what we are doing is communicating with itsy bitsy intelligent creatures who live in and around us infinitely. In fact, one could argue that we are their creations with DNA as their constructs. They make up what we are."

"Man, you are crazy," Dickie told Hoss.

"Why not then?"

"Whatever. Why not?"

Paranoia

I guess I am just a paranoid pharmacist. I go to work six days a week and make above average earnings legitimately, yet I am still compelled to sell pills illegally. It is really getting to me. I have to quit soon before I get busted. Dickie thinks we are all safe, but I have heard, 'The more you gamble the more you have to lose'. We have been gambling a number of years now.

We are asking for it, ya know, disdaining the law. How am I going break it to the guys? They are going to be mad. I must tell them soon.

Soon.

Equality

“Yeah, I met this girl downtown the other night. She came over to my crib last night and she went straight to dick suckin’,” said Dickie.

“Really?”

“Yeah man,” affirmed Dickie. “Twice.”

“Twice in a row?”

“Twice in a row.” Dickie broke a wide smile telling this, “She said she’s had a crush on me for years.”

“Sounds cushy.”

“Super cushy! She kissed on me for a couple minutes and then down on her knees. Personally, I don’t think my knees could take all that kneeling, but she did it with no problem. Like she had on knee pads.”

“How long?”

“Five minutes the first time,” Dickie bragged, “and ten minutes the second time.”

“Ha ha ha!” laughed his fellow officer. “Maybe she has a friend for me?”

“I don’t know man.”

“Shoo.”

“Man she got me hot!”

“Maybe she’ll do you too?’

La Cuenta

"Okay, so all together you owe me two thousand seven hundred balls," said Hoss as plainly as possible. Business ya know.

"Here you go dude."

"Super." The cash was in Hoss' hand. "Alright Kong, let's go."

"Cool." Kong was Hoss' protection. He is six foot five and two hundred and seventy pounds. Kong accompanies Hoss on most of the deals he makes. Kong has been tight with Hoss for just over three years. They cruise Adams Morgan together as well as any other night spot they hear is kickin'.

One time, about a year prior, Kong saved Hoss' life. Kong took a bullet in his arm before disarming the guy and breaking his arm, a compound fracture. That guy is lucky Kong did not break his neck, but Hoss says they are not in the killing business.

No one generally tries to get over on Hoss. If they do, Kong straightens them out.

Vacation

Saul Biggs again.

"I've got a reliable source telling me we will get results Chief, if we begin surveillance on them," Saul told the head man.

"Okay Saul, I'll give you a team to coordinate. Does that satisfy you?"

"Definitely. When can I start?"

"It'll take about a week to get things rolling, so I'll say middle of next week."

"In the meantime…" Saul tried to say.

"In the meantime why don't you relax until this thing gets going," said the Chief.

"Alright."

"Why don't you take your wife and son on a brief trip."

"But…"

"Don't worry, the bad guys will still be here when you get back." Saul stood speechless as the Chief began to shuffle papers. "That's all."

"Thanks John," Saul said and then exited the office.

Lights

"Oh shit! It's the cops." There were flashing lights pulling quickly in behind them. Hoss pulled over. It was night. The cop turned her spotlight on them. They quietly sat for a minute. Hoss got out his license and registration and rolled down his window. The officer approached.

"May I see your license and registration?"

"Here ya go." Hoss handed her his credentials.

"Do you know why I stopped you?" As she said this another cop pulled in behind them.

"No ma'am."

"Your tail lights are out."

"Oh really? I had no idea."

"Yes. I'll be back in a moment." As she said this, a third police car pulled up behind them. The cop walked back to her car where the other officers greeted her. Hoss and his buddy sat silently. Minutes later she came back with a clipboard in hand. She spoke.

"I have a citation for defective equipment here. By signing this it is not an admission of guilt. You are simply agreeing to appear in court or pre-pay the fine. This is a pre-payable offense so you do not have to go to court for this. Is that all clear to you?"

"Yes ma'am." She handed Hoss the clipboard, pointing to the X where he needed to sign.

"Sign here please." Hoss signed. "If you decide to contest this you can come to court on the written date, okay?"

"Yes ma'am."

"Alright, where are you headed?"

"Home."

"You should turn on your blinking hazard lights so other drivers can see you. Okay?"

"Yeah."

"Have a safe evening," said the lady officer.

And that was that.

Sleep

"Can I get another beer?" Hoss asked his hostess, Jennifer. She came back with two. She said nothing. That night Jennifer was driving Hoss home.

"You know, you seem older when you're more relaxed," she told him. She looked at Hoss as she said this. She liked to look at Hoss. He liked to look at her too.

"Ya think?"

"Yeah."

"Did I ever tell you I was in a mental hospital once?" Hoss queried.

"No."

"I'd been awake for days and I thought I was part of the movies that I watched. I thought they were about me," Hoss revealed.

"Yeah, when I was in college," Jennifer related, "art college, every few months we'd stay up for days at a time. The trick was to keep busy."

"Oh."

"But yeah," Jennifer continued, "we hallucinated too."

Miracle

I'm afraid people are reading my mail before it gets to me. I am Schmerrer. Why am I afraid? After all, they are postcards. But I am very afraid, kind of like being scared of the dark. That was before Zillia.

Zillia is one of many pills I stock in my pharmacy. It is a black triangular pill, good for anxiety among other things. I take one a day now, every day, I have lost my anxious fears, for the most part anyhow. Or so I think.

But these side effects are developing. It's okay though because a doctor prescribed it.

North East West South

Schmerrer closed his eyes and then became subconscious. He was in downtown Washington D.C. on the Mall with Hoss and Dickie. They were walking up the sidewalk on Constitution Avenue. Schmerrer spoke.

“Guys, I’m gonna stop getting pills from China.”

“What?” blasted Dickie.

“C’mon Schmerrer. What’s wrong?” asked Hoss.

“I just feel like we’re pushing our luck and besides, I think most of the drugs we sell go to kids.”

“So,” said a blistered Dickie.

“If that’s true man, they’re gonna get ‘em whether we sell ‘em or somebody else does,” Hoss reasoned.

“So be it, but I don’t want to be responsible for ruining kids’ lives.”

“Man!” zooked Dickie.

“Let’s race for it,” suggested Hoss.

“What?” asked Schmerrer, but it was too late. Hoss and Dickie were gone running like streaks of light. Schmerrer tried to follow, but his feet were too heavy. Too heavy now to even walk. Suddenly, as if he blinked, everything went pitch black.

Schmerrer awoke startled. The dream had been so real. His friends helped him to his feet.

Luxury

"The weather here is so pleasant," said Eileen to her husband Saul.

"Yes dear," replies Saul.

"You know what I'd like to do tomorrow?"

"What dear?"

"I want to ride jet skis."

"We can do that." And then they lay silent on their reclined chairs under an umbrella as their child played on the beach of Destin, Florida.

Barker

Drugs! Drugs! I got 'em! Who needs 'em? I can get any pill, as long as you're willing to pay. I've got the supply for you to buy. Adults! Kids! I don't care. Get everything you want to get out of your skin. The situation is win win win! Some come all you players. I've got the game of your life. See how much you can do. One hit. Two hits. Three hits. Four. Look in your mind and open the door. The door to free thinking. True liberty for you. The ideal American way. What more needs to be said? Hey, come on. This is fun. The most fun you'll ever have. Yeah!

Life should be a party and you are invited. Whoop it up because you might be dead tomorrow. Celebrate! Celebrate! Ra ra ra! Sis boom bah! Buy 'em in quantity and put yourself into business. You there! Do you want to be the coolest of all your friends? Become a dealer and I'll make it worth your while! Alright! Alright! Step right up and I will take your orders.

The Bowl

"That guy shreds."

"Yup."

Hoss and Dickie were out at Lake Fairfax riding the skateboard park. Hoss's bodyguard lurked in the background. He did not skate.

"I need some water."

"I hear that." Hoss and Dickie made their way across the park to the sidelines where their stuff was, where their water was. They decided to wrap it up. The two had been skating the bowl for two hours, which they felt confident they could ride without breaking any bones. Staying away from the big ramps and the huge hills showed wisdom. Hoss has broken both ankles skating and Dickie two fingers.

That was when they were younger and more reckless. Nowadays they could not afford to be laid up with injuries.

1996

Schmerrer was there at the 1996 Olympics in Atlanta at the park when the bomb blew up. He remembers. He told his date about it…

"I was watching the band whilst having a beer some fifty yards from the stage. All of a sudden there was a canon-like kaboom. I felt the shockwave almost instantly. I saw a woman with blood spattered across the front of her white shirt.

I walked up to the front of the stage. The light show kept its pace with pre-programmed spotlights flashing hither and yon on the audience. The band stopped. People quickly thinned out and then the police started to evacuate the park. I watched the mayhem for as long as possible from the railing that partitioned off the stage from the crowd. Then I was asked by security to leave.

It was incredible," Schmerrer finished up. His date listened intently.

"Weren't you scared?" she asked.

"There really wasn't enough time to be scared. It all happened so quick, but I'll tell ya, I was this close to death," he said as he held up his hands mimicking a short distance.

Schmerrer's family had been scammed along with hundreds of others. They had paid for a residence through the Apple Tree Company. When they arrived in town, the house he had rented for the three week stint was still occupied. The home owners said they never received payment for the time and so they decided to stay in town for the international event.

Schmerrer was angered. What did they mean they never got paid? His family paid six thousand dollars to the rental company, Apple Tree.

“Well,” they said, “we never got paid.” So Schmerrer, like hundreds of others, had to find alternate housing. Hundreds had been scammed who thought they had housing. All Apple Tree did was keep the money.

He made the best of it. Many of them were housed at a civic center on cots and floor pads. He could have gone home, but he wanted to stay. He saw swimming, gymnastics and basketball. A memory so wonderful.

Sight

People with glasses talk more. People with twenty twenty sight are more sight-sensual. But do not listen to me, listen to the story.

Be happy if you can see. Be happy if someone else can help you see. Many will never see,

I-95

Hoss and Kong were cruising south on Interstate 95 out of D.C. Kong had the killer bud. They smoked a bowl and then another. Hoss sprayed deodorizer which they let do its thing with their windows rolled up. After a couple minutes they rolled down their windows.

Hoss was driving. He jumped in with a pack of speeders doing eighty five miles per hour. In his highness, he did not take much note that he was the last in the pack.

Minutes later. Waaaoooh! Waaaoooh! The flashing lights and the siren. They were being pulled over. Hoss parked it on the side of the highway and turned the music off. The officer approached.

"Howdy," Hoss said.

"Hi," replied the officer. "You know why I stopped you?"

"Yeah, I was goin' too fast."

"Have you had anything to drink tonight?"

"Just a soda."

"Alright, can I get your license and registration?" Hoss gave it to him. The officer went to his car and momentarily returned.

"Could you step out of your vehicle and follow me?" Hoss got out and followed the officer. He had to empty his pockets and be searched. After that…

"Get in on the other side," said the cop as he got in the cruiser. High as clouds, Hoss sat with the officer for what seemed like fifteen minutes. The officer checked Hoss' identification on his computer. He was issued a citation for speeding. "You know I could give you a reckless driving citation, but you seem to be going along okay, just too fast."

"Yes sir." Kong was sure he was next and that there would be someone coming to take them both away for the grass, but nope.

"Alright," said the policeman, "slow it down and be safe."

Blind

"Did you hear about the new 'Mandate Law'?" Richard was asked at work.

"Naw."

"All U.S. students have to be registered with the government all the way down as far as pre-school. Fingerprints, eye scans, DNA, and everything."

"What, all public school kids?" Richard asked.

"Yeah," said his colleague.

"Sounds a bit totalitarian," reflected Richard.

"No. It is for their benefit, their safety."

"Oh, I get it," Richard said, but he did not really.

Discernment

"Shooot, y'all wanna see something? Kong, show these ladies your back. Heh heh," laughed Hoss. Kong lifted his shirt revealing bulky musculature and also a large tattooed dragon face about sixteen inches in diameter.

"That's cool!" cooed one girl. The other said nothing. These chicks were cold. Hoss dug it. Kong did too. Soon enough they were chatting away and drinking beers and shots. They got warm. They took taxis home that night, ladies in tow. Understand?

High School Games

Richard was back, the last football game of the season. He was still in cahoots with his teenage sweetheart. She fancied that she would one day marry Richard. Richard fancied he might have sex with her and nothing more. Dick or realist?

"Hi!" she exclaimed with a big smile.

"What's up."

"What are you doing after the game?" she asked.

"You," he said with a straight face.

"You're so bad."

"Badder than a Smokey Mountain bear." She laughed. "So will I see you after the game?" he probed.

"Do ya want to?"

"Yeah."

"Then you will." This made Richard hum with energy.

The game went by quickly and there were no altercations for Richard to control. As the crowd thinned out Richard grew enwrapped with anticipation. His girl was inside changing. He talked shop with the other two cops at the front gate. They did not know of his lustful plans and they never would. Richard was good at keeping his mouth shut.

Ten minutes passed and Richard sat in his squad car awaiting his little lady's emergence from the locker room. And there she was, an apex of beauty.

Richard drove to the back of the parking lot. She followed on foot and then hopped in.

“Where to?” he asked.

“How ‘bout a hotel?” she asked with wild eyes.

“Right on,” he said keeping his composure. He drove. He had already had a hotel in mind. It was actually an unoriginally named place called ‘Richmond Motel’. Rooms were the cheapest around, forty dollars plus tax. As they pulled into the parking lot, Richard picked up the mic to his radio.

“Hi Julie, This is Richard Hill. I’ve got a situation on my hands and have to go home for an hour or so.”

“Roger. What’s the emergency?” asked Julie from the speaker.

“No emergency. Just a little private personal thing. I’ll call you when I’m done.”

“Ten four,” said Julie the dispatcher. Richard turned off the radio. His date chimed in.

“Only an hour?”

“Sorry, but that’s all the time I’ve got tonight.”

“I guess we’ll have to make due.”

Veils

"The last thing we imported from England is punk rock music," said Cristina.

"Well, let's get outta here like spilt beer," replied Hoss. He listened to Imelda without judgment. He just liked being around her. She is one of Hoss' girlfriends. He has three regular girlfriends. Their names are Imelda, Jessica, and Gretchen.

Imelda is a hair design student. Jessica works with computers and Gretchen is a ceramicist from Sweden. As you might surmise, Hoss lives life in a delicate balance.

None of the ladies know about each other, but they all know he is a drug dealer. They all get a thrill from being with an outlaw. They all think that he is so busy he has little time to spend with them. Now one was pregnant.

Does Hoss ever feel he is being unfair to his women?

Never.

E-Dress

"Taking a shit while you're trippin' is the weirdest." Dickie smiled as he related his opinion, "It's like you're losing part of yourself."

"I can't see it, but I definitely need to get your new e-dress," said Hoss into his two-way.

"seventytwobull@always.com"

"Thanks. I gotta dig at you sometime next week."

"Later Hoss."

"Later Dickie." They hung up. Then Hoss got into the store. He was looking for some jewelry for his sister's birthday. He wanted a jade bracelet, common in Asian cultures.

"Hi. My name is Hoss. May I pleases see that bracelet," he said as he pointed.

"Nice to meet you Hoss," said the woman with an arched back and a glowing Chinese grin. No doubt she was a hottie.

"Yes, that one," he said and instantly was appeased. He held the bracelet in his hand and wondered if it would fit. "If it doesn't fit can I exchange it?"

"Of course," she smiled.

On Richard's end, he received a call on his squawk-box, "We have a report of drag racing on Jeff-Davis highway."

"On it like a stain," replied Dickie into his mic. He was gone.

Freezing

It was cold enough to see your breath. That was the cue for Winter to begin soon, bare branches everywhere outside. The days grew shorter and shorter. Richard and Hoss were confident all was well. They did not listen to the qualms of their friend and business partner. Schmerrer's concern grew every day. He was sure they were going to get caught soon. Sure, deep down inside he felt small up into all his extremities.

Schmerrer felt like a polluted stagnant pond, full of muckerslime. A pool of slappyknacker. He wanted out and he knew they did not feel the same way.

What could he do?

What would he do?

Profits

Business was good.

"I'm tellin' ya, we could double our endeavors."

"Well I'm all for it," said Dickie to Hoss. "We'll talk to Schmerrer about it tomorrow, okay?"

"Yeah man." Hoss stood up and headed for the kitchen.

"Could you grab me another beer?"

"I'm already on it." Fifteen seconds later Hoss was back. "Last two," Hoss iterated.

"I'll go to the store after these."

"I'll go with you." They finished their beers while watching boxing on the tube.

"You ready?" asked Dickie.

"Yulp." They had not noticed it had begun raining. Dickie opened the front door.

"Man! It's pouring!"

"Big time," Hoss agreed. They dashed to the car. The windshield clouded with their breath. Dickie turned on the ignition. It sputtered then started. Hoss cranked the defroster not yet warmed by the engine. It still began to clear the windshield. They sat quietly, waiting for visibility. Dickie clicked on the radio. 'The End' by the Doors was playing. They listened, not speaking.

It had not rained for a couple of weeks. It seemed like evening with all the clouds, even though it was two thirty in the afternoon. Dickie grew impatient. He cleared a whole in the fogged glass with his sleeve, turned on his windshield wipers and lights. They buckled their seat belts and were off.

Fate happened. Dickie was pushing fifty-five in a forty mile per hour zone. The car began to pivot on the slick street. Dickie tried to compensate by turning the wheel a little to the left and hitting the gas. It was a little too much.

The car jerked to the left.

"What are you doing?" belted Hoss.

"We're hydroplaning!" Dickie frantically replied. They jumped the median's curb into oncoming traffic. Coming directly at them was an eighteen wheeler speeding above the limit. Dickie prayed to GOD. Hoss prayed too. It was not enough.

In an instant, Dickie was killed as they impacted with the huge truck. It cut the car nearly in half lengthwise leaving Hoss alive, uninjured, and mortified.

Funeral

The ground was cold and solid hard under their feet, sadness all around. They were burying Officer Richard Hill, complete with a twenty one gun salute.

It was a closed casket event, basically because Dickie's remains were in multiple pieces. Dickie's mom wept uncontrollably as guests paid their respects. Hoss and Schmerrer knew him best perhaps. They each gave Dickie's mom a hug and then they were out the door to eat at Third Street.

They had coffee and sandwiches. Schmerrer spoke first after eating.

"I guess we're done then," he said with relief.

"What are you talking about?" asked Hoss. Schmerrer leaned in close to reply.

"The business."

"What?"

"We no longer have an inside man. Doesn't that make us done?"

"Are you serious?"

"Yeah."

"Look Schmerrer, we can do it without him. I'm as sad as the next guy that he is gone, but we still have a very viable prospect. Don't you think everything is going smooth?"

"I just assumed it was a three man team. Now we are only two. Doesn't that scare you?"

"All I know is the money is great. And since Dick is gone we will each have more. Can't you see that?"

"Yeah, but is jail worth it?"

"Neither of us has gone to jail yet and I don't plan on it."

"I don't plan on it either, but I don't think anyone plans on going to jail. We are in a dangerous situation," Schmerrer said in a hushed tone leaning close to Hoss again. "Can't you see that?"

"As far as I am concerned everything is fine." Schmerrer said nothing. "Look," Hoss continued, "we can keep our current level of business. You know I wanted to expand, but maybe that isn't such a good idea for now."

"That's definitely true."

"Buy why quit? We've had no scares in the past."

"Look, I'm scared every day. I've got a great job with great pay. I feel like I'm being greedy. I mean, ninety grand a year is plenty to live on."

"Yeah, but wouldn't you like to retire early?"

"It's not about that. I just don't want to ruin my life for a few extra bux."

"It's more than that."

"Yeah, but I just don't think it's worth it anymore."

"Come on Schmerrer. Where's that wild spirit bro?"

"It has matured to a form of caution. I used to know no boundaries, but now I feel them. With Dickie gone just like that I feel mortal. Very mortal! I want to settle down. Me and my big ego has been taught a lesson."

"What's that?"

"Not to be so brash. Don't you feel it too?"

"Nope," replied Hoss.

"Well I do and I have to listen to myself. I can't keep doing what I know could ruin my life."

"Won't you miss the excitement? Doesn't being just a pharmacist sound boring to you?"

"Doesn't an eight by ten cell sound boring?"

"What about all those people who depend on us to keep their lives exciting and fun?"

"Maybe they'll wake up too."

"Or maybe someone else will take up our market, a market I've worked hard to create."

"So be it."

"Look, maybe you just need a few days to reflect, mull things over."

"You know this isn't just because Dickie is dead. You know I've been talking about this for a while."

"Man. How can you give up?"

"I just have to." At that moment their pie arrived. Time to chow.

Severance

"We live in a hostile environment," said the newsman on the teevee. "In Washington D.C. there were two hundred and fifty six murders last year. The facts cannot be dismissed." That was enough for Schmerrer. He turned off his set and went upstairs to get ready for bed.

After a hot bath, he pulled back his covers and climbed into bed. It was another day done, two days after the funeral. Schmerrer thought how he would never see his friend again. He thought of Hoss and how he did not want to quit selling pills illegally. They were once perfect, he thought. A cop. A pharmacist. And a drug dealer. They were once undefeatable. Now they were not. Though Schmerrer's thoughts were racing, he had put in an eleven hour day at work and soon was fast asleep.

Impasse

Here we are at an impasse. Hoss and Schmerrer are in disagreement. The story of three friends is now a story of two. Life now seemed shorter and while one sees life as delicate, the other sees it as a tiger. Who will prevail, convincing the other of their path? Or, seeing their disagreement, would their paths diverge?

Connectivity

The telephone jingled.

"Yo," answered Hoss.

"We need to connect," said the other end.

"How about tonight at Madam's Organ?"

"Cool. What time?"

"Ten okay?"

"Yeah."

"Alright. Later."

"Peace." They hung up. Hoss kept the receiver in hand and dialed a number.

"Carla here," she answered.

"Hi Carla. This is Hoss calling. "I met you two weeks ago at Sting (a weekly dance party)."

"Yeah, how've you been?"

"Good. And you?"

"I'm doin' well. Just working a lot."

"Me too."

"I'm coming into D.C. tonight and was wondering if you wanted to hang out."

"It's Tuesday."

"Yeah and I know it's short notice, but…"

"I think I can make it. What did you have in mind?"

“I’m supposed to meet a friend in Adam’s Morgan at Madam’s Organ around ten.”

“Uh huh.”

“So I was thinking we could meet there around eleven and then maybe go dancing somewhere.”

“Eleven’s so late.”

“How about ten?”

“That’s probably better.”

“So ten?”

“Yeah.”

“Okay, I look forward to seeing you.”

“Me too.”

“Bye.”

“Bye.” Hoss hung up the phone letting her speak last. He always tried to let women speak last.

Landscaping

That night.

"Can you keep a secret?" Hoss asked.

"Yeah."

"I'm nuts. Wanna know why?"

"Why?"

"I cut grass all day."

"Is that why you're so tan?" Carla asked Hoss.

"Yulp."

"I like that."

"But here's my secret," Hoss said quietly. "I'm a drug dealer." He grinned. "Wanna know another secret?"

"Yeah."

"I guess it's not much of a secret, but you are so smokin'." She giggled. "Now check it…" Hoss noticed she was looking into space. She recognized him nil. He collected himself. "Do you like to cook?"

She looked him in the eyes and thought, what?

"Do you like to cook?" he repeated.

"Yeah," which she followed with another chuckle.

Thinking

“Alcohol is for talking I think,” said Hoss.

“So, have you thought about what we talked about the other day?” Schmerrer asked Hoss.

“Yeah. I’ve been rattlin’ that around.” He paused then raised his eyebrows in earnest. “Do you remember our gym teachers Fred and Barney?”

“From high school?”

“Yeah.”

“Yeah.”

“Those guys never see the kinda money we make in a year, and GOD bless him, with Dickie gone it rings up even higher.”

“No Hoss. That’s not what I care about. Don’t you see? With Dickie gone we have no protection from the inside. No guy to keep us a step ahead.”

“So it’s over?”

“It’s gotta be.”

“Over huh?” Hoss then got a flash and continued, “You sure you don’t want to go get hookers like we did when we were sixteen?”

“I’m telling you, I have no heart left for this.”

That was it. No more wads of cash.

Get Away

Hoss had to get away. Schmerrer did not want to go. Hoss told his regular girlfriends he had to go away on business, something about new lawnmower technology. In fact, Hoss asked Carla to go with him to the Caribbean.

She said 'Yes!'

Eight days into his getaway, Hoss received a text message that his girlfriend had a miscarriage. His baby, which was a boy, had been lost.

Dickie's Incomplete Account entitled 'Whiplash'

Hoss, Schmerrer and I are best pals. Comrades. Ever since middle school we have hung out. Schmerrer is two years older, but we treat each other equally. We were sort of leaders of our clique. We hung out at the shopping center. There were so many in our clique. On an average day you could find five to twenty five of us hanging out on the benches smoking cigs, bumming change, and doing a lot of spitting.

They call me Dickie, but my given name is Richard. I am the first to begin drinking alcohol. In fifth grade I made a suicide which is a splash from each of my folks liquor bottles. Bombs away. I found out what getting wasted was like at an early age. I told my neighbor, Schmerrer, about it later. Schmerrer was intrigued and the next week us two snuck out in the middle of the night and proceeded to get trashed. Soon enough, we included Hoss getting trashed. We threw rocks at windows and ran away. It was a blast.

By middle school, we were getting toasted a lot. It was around that time when Hoss' older sister got us stoned. So you are looking at three kids, two fourteen and one almost sixteen, who went to school, but whose real passion was getting intoxicated.

Come Schmerrer's high school graduation he enrolled at Virginia Commonwealth University where he began a track in biology. Of all things, he wanted to be a pharmacist. Unlike Schmerrer, Hoss and I did not know what we wanted, but we knew it had to be exciting like taking LSD before school or jumping off a forty foot cliff into water. We had two more years to decide. Above all, we knew we were hometown kids.

Years later I am twenty four as is Hoss. Hoss legitimately has a landscaping business employing eleven people other than himself. I am a cop. Now we also have Schmerrer.

He is what he wants to be, even has his own drug store. So we all are functional adults in the community. But beneath the surface we are players in a much more serious game. You see, we are criminals. We are a crime triumvirate. We sell pills.

Schmerrer gets the drugs from various international sources. I keep an car on the inside with the police and Hoss is the actual dealer. We have all the bases covered or so we think.

Naje Sibe is on the case. She works undercover tracking criminals nationwide. If she has her way she will lock us up along with every other bad guy out here.

"Fight 'til Death!" is her motto on her office wall, professionally designed and written by a calligrapher. Naje is hot headed and full of righteousness. As she sees it, she has never done anything bad in her life, seeing herself as a guardian of goodness and truth.

Naje rarely drank alcohol and never in excess. The only drugs she has ever taken were prescribed from an doctor. Naje has a strong holy faith and attends Sunday church whenever she can as work permits. I know about her and feed her false information.

I am checking providence and open to a random page in my Bible. Ezekiel 33. I read, "I do not enjoy seeing a sinner die. I would rather he stop sinning and live." Interesting. I wonder why good people across the globe are suffering.

? Dickie's account of this story ends here and so it ends this writing ʕ

Intermission

My life truly started out in a suburban town, a planned community. In fact, it was the first planned community founded on the New York City real estate money of Robert E. Simon. It is Reston, Virginia. I experienced a brain injury when I was about 13 years old from a downhill skateboarding accident in 1985. I was moving at high speed down a major hill along on my way home from a friend's house on a hot summer day when I hit a crack in the sidewalk. The accident left me unconscious on the side of the road having seizures as rush hour traffic drove by. Granted this was 1985 and there was no such thing as a cell phone.

I awoke in an ambulance. The EMT told me a passer-by had called from a pay phone to report my condition to authorities. Maybe they had called 911? I never found out who reported the situation to the emergency team. They took me by ambulance to the local medical treatment facility which was not a hospital. It was there that I received medical care until my mother and father arrived separately to see what had happened to me. My parents were divorced and each arrived in their own time to be told by doctors that I had suffered a concussion and been found unconscious having convulsions on the roadside. There was little concern and then I went home with my mother.

I do not remember everything about my childhood, but in retrospect it was this event that changed me. I lost touch with lots of friends and at my own birthday party the following year I did not even want to be there. My circle of friends changed and I became increasingly divergent from mainstream social interactions. I was depressed and often thought of suicide. My family was strangling me in more ways than one, especially when they turned a blind eye to me being sexually abused by my mother's boyfriend's son, and I lost faith in society. I saw through the fake standards that were espoused in school, by the media, and in religion. My faith was gone.

Hardcore punk music had messages of honesty and carried over into early rap music. They told truths and exposed the fallacies of our United States systems, and really the wider world. Alcohol, cigarettes, cannabis, and other drugs were introduced to me and I took them happily. They made me feel alive and living, after all I had been wanting to die for years. However, there is a catch.

Recently a source confirmed my fears that have been brewing for years. Cheap weed (cannabis) called "swag" was the staple for all the kids and that carried over into my college years. I could get an ounce of this for $100. Once I even bought a quarter pound of swag for $250. I thought that was great and even if I could get "kind bud" (today it would be referenced as medical cannabis), I bought swag because of the volume for less money. A quarter ounce of kind bud would be $100 to $125 and the difference was clear. More weed, but less quality. Here is the catch. Swag has chemicals sprayed on it by the thugs who source it out to dealers, whether they be inner city thugs or foreign entities. They sprayed debilitating things on the weed, including PCP I am told, to addict me and destroy my brain. And they were doing this nationwide and still do today. Poor people can afford this and it is everywhere. The war on drugs became a war on the customers to keep us addicted, cloud our judgement, and in the process cause us chemical induced mental illness.

Doctors say cannabis causes mental illness and the public believes it. This is the same source that says cannabis has no medical value and allows our government to classify it as a Class 1 drug alongside heroin and other severely toxic drugs. The foreign compounds sprayed on swag weed and then consumed unknowingly by the public has been causing mental illness outcomes for years for multitudes of people. Fast forward to now. I was diagnosed with a mental health illness in 1998 and have been taking Zyprexa since then as an atypical antipsychotic. Psychiatrists say it is one of the best pharmaceutical drugs for treatment of schizophrenia and bi-polar disorder. It causes extreme side effects, leading some to diabetes and in my case, I gained 100 pounds and slept for 20 hours a day for many years.

Now it is 2018 and I have been taking this drug for 20 years. As I have recently come to terms with being sexually molested growing up, awakening to my family being enablers of these crimes, and becoming independent, I feel my diagnosis was incorrect and not valid. With the recent confirmation that the swag cannabis I smoked for years was tainted with poison unnatural additives by nefarious thugs who controlled my supply to control me and harm me, I am certain that my diagnosis was invalid. And as my life currently stands I have been titrating down to eventually end the use of Zyprexa aka olanzapine. This is where it gets tough.

My current dose is now 2.5mg (I was blindsided when hospitalized starting with 15 mg a day in 1998) and I am starting to feel withdrawals from Zyprexa such as sleeplessness, nausea, headaches, sweating, lack of appetite, body aches, and general feelings of uneasiness. Tonight, I read about these exact symptoms as reported by others who have stopped this medication. As I move to cessation, these symptoms are expected to increase into possible sleeplessness for multiple weeks and further intensification to include vomiting daily. That sounds a lot like an opioid withdrawal and I am scared. Now listen to this this.

I watched Weed 4 on CNN on April 29, 2018 and Dr. Sanjay Gupta reported evidence that says medical cannabis can alleviate these withdrawal symptoms and repair my injured brain. Yes, that is his stated facts. Dr. Gupta reports science confirms these as facts. I have long believed in the positive efficacy of cannabis and have not smoked swag for years. I would truly like to obtain and consume medical cannabis as I move through withdrawal from the antipsychotic drug Zyprexa which is reported to be very debilitating upon full cessation. I also want to benefit from the healing and rejuvenation capacities that cannabis can provide to my injured brain. I live in Virginia and cannabis is still illegal here. My job is a drug free workplace and I rely on my earnings to support my family. My wife cannot work much due to disabilities and she has expensive medical needs. As my reading indicates, I anticipate facing ongoing physically painful withdrawal from Zyprexa and readjustment without the aforementioned proven natural plant assistance. I know cannabis could help me and yet if I use it then I could lose my job and possibly go to jail. This is most troubling, especially because an hour to the north in Washington DC cannabis is fully legal and decriminalized.

This means I could become homeless, lose my car, not have food, and live in a tent or at a shelter for using this powerful natural medicine called cannabis. I could lose my family and not be able to support myself. All because this historically and recently scientifically proven beneficial natural medicine is illegal for reasons that I do not understand. It has helped people throughout history and was legal here in the United States of America until the 1930's. I face possibly debilitating effects as I move to end my dependence on Zyprexa, a drug that was basically forced upon me in a time of weakness, and my government does not even care to validate my well being or that of millions of others who face pharmaceutical addictions caused by doctors. Cannabis could benefit us all. When can I enjoy cannabis to help me in my struggle and all those others who are looking down the barrel of a loaded gun from which this plant could save us all?

This my friend is the swag weed dilemma.

And this is why I am in dire straits with my government as they have proclaimed a war on drugs. A war against me. A war against our medicine.

**I sent this letter to my Virginia Senators Kaine and Warner in the late Spring of 2018 for help. Senator Kaine's written response was an eye-opening blessing. I was grateful his office responded in his name.

HORIZON REALIZED

HORIZON REALIZED

He wants to know what is real. For that he yearns. He wants to know why there is life. To inner-space and outer-space he travels and yet, perhaps, remembers none.

If he sleeps is he awake? If he could just know then he could impress the World. Tonight will be different from all other nights. He is a young American white boy.

And so we peer in for a slice…

A thief. A liar. A cheater. He was all those things. To his Mom. To his Dad. It was all taboo and he did it all. Fighting. Cussing. Smoking. It was all cool. What didn't he do? Drinking. Tripping. Huffing. All was fair game.

He did well in school. He did well in art class. He did well in biology and math. Calculus in high school. Sure. He went to college, but that is not the tale I tell. That was all elementary. It was his private life in which he was a criminal.

And he did it so well.

"I'll meet you at the front door." He had just climbed in a back window to a house and his partner walked around front. It was two o'clock on a hot summer afternoon. He climbed into the house through a second story window off of a ladder which they found in the back yard. They were down for some looting. They had knocked on the front door repeatedly to make sure no one was home. There was a car in the driveway. They knocked. No one answered. They tried walking in the front door, but it was locked so they went around back. That was where they saw the open window.

He did not know why he broke into the house, nor did his bro. He guessed it was for the money, perhaps beer, or a bicicle. It could have been any reason. Television had lost its edge. He could even predict what the characters were going to say. The movie channels were good, but he generally watched movies at night while getting juiced on cola sodas. Caffeine was good, he thought. Plus there was all that sugar. Mmmmm! Sugar. Ice cream fit the bill too. These were things his Mom kept in stock for him. His friends liked to come over because their houses never had as many goodies as his. He saw that they used him, but that did not matter he figured because everyone uses people.

For him, he used them for live entertainment. He hung out with the jokesters, many of whom would drop-out of school in years to come. Some would move away. He remembered Curtis, Marc, and Sean from kindergarten to the third grade. They were great pals. They called themselves “the Crazies”. But then they moved away. He had not seen them for years and doubted he would ever see them again.

He walked downstairs to the front door and opened it; his pal marched right in.

“I’ll check the fridge,” said his mate.

“I’m goin’ upstairs,” he said. He did not look in the jewelry box on the dresser. Instead he looked in the drawers for cash, not thinking about stealing items to pawn. All he wanted was moolah. Casheesh. And that he found. There were three twenties in an envelope in a desk drawer. He and his buddy had a deal. They split everything fifty-fifty. That was thirty bucks for him. Meantime, downstairs his bro was filling his backpack full of beer. They were only thirteen and they were going to get drunk off their stolen treasure.

They would stay up until two or three AM and sneak out while his parents slept. They snuck out all the time to walk through paved pathways linking the neighborhoods of their community together. There was only one hazard. Cops. They hated cops.

Police harassed them all the time for hanging out at shopping centers, strip mall shopping centers. Sometimes as many as thirty kids hung out, bumming change, smoking cigarettes, and doing a lot of spitting. During the day, if they skipped school, they would hang out in the woods or at someone's house whose parents both worked. In the after school hours they hung out at various shopping centers or went out swimming at the nearby lake. Today there was no school, just a lot of free-time to kill. And so they were in this house, rummaging through these people's personal belongings.

After taking all the beer, his friend put his backpack by the front door and went upstairs.

"Yo, where are ya?"

"In here." He went in there.

"Did ya check any of these other rooms yet?"

"I've been through the room with the 'Do Not Enter' sign on it, but not the other two."

"I'm on it." They left the house a little richer, a little bolder, and a little braver.

That is not our story. We need to go back earlier, for before his teens, when Sail embarked into badness.

"Sailaja, you left the computer on again," called his mother. "You know you're supposed to turn it off during thunderstorms." Sailaja laughed as he pulled the arm off his plastic spaceman.

And here is where we find our story with Sailaja at five years old, just the beginning of Sailaja's troublemaking.

"Maaaama, can I have more bacon?" he asked with disdain.

"Sure thing dear." His Mama walked over to the table and put three more slices of bacon on his plate. His Father read the newspaper while paying little attention to his Wife and Son. As soon as his Mom looked the other way Sailaja dropped the bacon to the floor where his dog quickly munched them down. Sailaja snickered. His Mom turned and looked.

"What's so funny honey?" Sailaja raised his shoulders in query. His Dad now looked past his paper to his Son.

"You're the strong little one, aren't you." Sailaja grinned to his Poppa. Their dog stared intently at Sailaja. He knew he should not ask for more bacon because he had already gotten extra bacon twice.

"Mama, I'm done."

"Okay, Darling, you can go play." His Dad looked over his paper again at his boy who was getting out of his chair.

"Mom," his Dad said, "maybe we should take a trip to the pool later."

"Sure, Dad. How 'bout after lunch?" replied his Mom.

"Splendid." Dad paused then added, "Have I told you yet today how beautiful you are?"

"No."

"Well you are… gorgeous."

"Thank you dear," she said with a smile.

Sailaja went into his own playroom with their dog quick on his heels. Sailaja pushed the dog out the door and closed it so he was alone. He grabbed his gas station set-up and then took a car and rolled it in for a fill-up.

"That'll be eight dollars."

"Yes sir, here you go. Thank you." Then he moved that car out of the gas station. He rolled another car up to the pump and proceeded to give it some gas. Then he said, "That'll be seven dollars."

"Go to hell asshole," Sailaja said in a gruff voice and then rolled the car away as he mimicked a car peeling out. Then with one hand he flipped over the gas station. It hit the wall with a crash.

From outside the room his Mama called, "Everything alright in there?"

"Yeah."

"Okay."

That was just the beginning. Next he grabbed a little ball and threw it against the window. It bounced back at him. He did not catch it, but he tried. Again and again he tossed it at the window. Sailaja got bored with that soon enough, so he lay down on his back and started kicking his legs. Next he got up and ran in circles. He began to shriek. "Aaah!" he hollered.

"Aaah!"

His Mom opened the door.

"You scared me. I thought you were hurt." Sailaja said nothing, but he bugged his eyes out and screamed again.

"Aaah!"

"Honey, please quiet down. For me, okay." Sailaja stopped his yelling. "I'm going to leave this door open, alright." Sailaja nodded and with that his Mom left the room. In came their dog who licked Sailaja's little face.

"No!" he said. "No!" he repeated as he pushed the dog away. Doggy stared as Sailaja picked up one of his toy metal cars. He tossed it, like the ball, at the window. The car fell to the ground. He grabbed a little metal backhoe and chucked it at the window.

Crash! The window cracked with a few shards hitting the floor.

"Sailaja!" called his Mom and she was there in an instant. "Sailaja, what are you doing?" He pointed at the window and gave a high pitched shriek. "Come with me," commanded Mom as she went to get the vacuum. "Your son just broke a window," said Mom to Dad. "Will you keep an eye on him while I clean up the glass?"

"Sure thing dear. Come sit on Daddy's lap son." And so he climbed upon his lap face to face. He began to pull on Daddy's mustache. His Dad told him, "Easy Son, easy." Then Sailaja pulled on his Daddy's lips. "Easy, Son, easy," his Daddy said.

It was later that day. Sailaja came in with his two friends Brian and Matt.

"Maaama!"

"Yes Sailaja?"

"Look what we found, Mama." Sailaja held up three small blue eggs. "The Mama bird won't take these back, will she, Mama?"

"That's right Sailaja."

"So can we eat them then?"

"I guess so." And so Sailaja, Brian, and Matt got to eat the robin eggs. His Mama cooked them sunny side up. They ate them with buttered toast.

"Maaama… can I go over to Brad's house?"

"Sure my Little Angel. Remember to look both ways before crossing the street."

"Okay, Maaama." And Sailaja was hop, skip, and jumping over to Brad's. Brad was in his driveway with Jason. Jason is the two and a half year old from next door. Big Sailaja sat right down with them in the gravel drive.

"Hi," said Brad.

"Hi," said Sailaja.

"Hyuh," said Jason.

"Jason. I bet you won't stick a rock up your nose," Sailaja said with raised eyebrows and a smile.

"Oh I wiw!" exclaimed Jason and with that, Jason stuck a rock up his left nostril.

"Ha!" Sailaja laughed.

"Ha haw!" laughed Brad. Jason tried to take the rock out but only drove it in further. Jason began to cry and rubbed his eyes. Then he began to wail.

“Jason, you better go home!” Sailaja commanded him. Brad and Sailaja laughed again and Jason went home.

The next day at Sailaja’s.

“Eat your cereal darling,” cooed his Mom.

“Okay, Maaama,” and he spooned a mouthful. He chewed. Then he spoke, “Maaama.”

“Yes, Sweetie?”

“I want to go to the park.”

“We can do that, dear, but after lunch.” Sailaja finished his breakfast and went up to his room. A few minutes passed.

“Honey!” she called him.

“Yes Maaama?”

“Do you want to play ‘Chutes and Ladders’?”

“Okay! I’ll be right there.” Sailaja knocked over all the blocks he had been stacking and rushed downstairs. He loved to play games with his Mother.

Sailaja loved to run and play, but Mama told him to sit still.

They went to the mall. There was a man preaching outside the doors as they walked in. “I am a priest of GOD’S revolution. I do not admire wealth unless it is the wealth of the mind, the soul, the spirit, whatever you call it. In the new world we will have no use for money, as all will share and be glorious. Respect will be…" And that is what they heard as they passed by and walked inside.

They were going to the Department of Motor Vehicles so Sailaja's Mom could update her driver's license picture. She did that every year. They waited in line for about fifteen minutes and were given the forms to fill out and a number letter combination, C514.

"Now serving C507 at window eight," came a voice over the intercom.

"Maaama."

"Yes Sailaja?"

"Can I please go play by the fountain?" He kicked his feet as they dangled off the chair. Waiting.

"I am sorry, Dear, but I cannot let you go play in the mall unsupervised."

"Unsupervised?"

"Yes, unsupervised Sailaja."

"But I want to."

"I'm sorry, but the answer is still no." Sailaja started to hum and dance in his seat.

"Sailajaaa."

"Yes, Mama?"

"Mind your manners."

"But I wanna play."

"You can play after we take care of my business here."

"Okay," said Sailaja with a frum.

"Remember to sit up straight and tall."

"Yes, Mama."

"Now serving C513 at window number two," came the voice over the intercom. Sailaja kept squirming so his Mama pulled him onto her lap. This calmed him down. He is always good when I hold him, Mama thought.

"Hello, Mother!" sang Dad as he entered the house.

"Hello, Father!" sang Mama.

"Where's my Little Man?"

"Here I am, Poppa!" sang Sailaja he came around the corner.

"How was work Dear?"

"Just perfect, Mother," said Dad as he hugged her. Sailaja got in on the hug too. Dad then picked him up. "Are we ready to go out to dinner?"

"I am! I am!" replied Sailaja.

"Yes Dear."

"We better bring umbrellas. There's a thunder storm on the way."

"Good thinking Daddy." Dad smiled.

"You know things couldn't be more perfect," said Mama. "What shall we eat tonight Sailaja?"

"Mexican! Mexican, Maaama!"

"Mexican it is!" boomed Dad and they were out the door. On their way there, Sailaja overheard his Father and Mother speaking.

"First they introduced bartender schooling ads in the media," Dad said. "Then once we had all the bars, then we created consumer related jobs. Then once we had all the service jobs lined up, we hyped up the information technology world and wa la, a booming system of classes from poor to rich interacting with very few new families, while gaining access to unimaginable wealth," finished Dad.

"You seem to be sharper since you've been taking that class, like you're getting something from it," said Mama. Sailaja heard them speak, but had little understanding of what they meant.

"You okay back there, youngster?"

"Yes I am, Poppa!"

"Shall we sing a song?" asked Mama as she looked back at Sailaja. He nodded.

"How about 'When the Saints go Marching In', Poppa?"

"Sounds good to me, Mama." Father glanced at them and they began to sing in unison. Sailaja was happy.

At eight years old, Sailaja began stealing from his parents. Dollars mostly. When Mom was not looking, he would snatch a bill or two from her purse. What was that for? He had so much that his parents gave him. Well here it is.

Candy and soda from the store up the street or from the ice cream truck that rolled through his subdivision a couple times a day. Mmmm, how he loved to sample the sugar products. It gave him so much energy. Mama did not give him sugary snacks besides soda and ice cream and there were so many others. No. She was into vegetables and fruits. Grilled cheese sandwiches were things which gave her boy calcium and protein and it had a good taste too. The closest she came to giving him other candy was letting him chew gum. That was the top, but for Sailaja it was only the beginning.

It acted as his gateway to other tooth decaying products. With the dollars he stole he bought candy bars and candy drops. Cookies. More soda and the soda gave him the most incredible rush. Oooo caffeine. Like a bee. Buzz. Buzz. So he had incredible secrets. Secrets a young boy should not have. He kept his secrets very well. He did not tell anyone how he stole. He just did it.

Let us go back again to five years old.

This particular Tuesday, mid-morning, Sailaja was urinating in the kitchen trash can while his mother sat in front of the Queen Latifah show on the television. Sailaja tinkled out the last bit. Then he ran into the living room shrieking.

"Aaaah! Aaaah!"

"Sailaja! Sailaja! What is it?" his Mama probed.

"Nothing, Maaama."

"Please quiet down, okay."

"Okay Maaama." Sailaja went to his room. He had a Batman car in which he put his Star Wars figures. They were his father's toys from when he was a boy. Completely cherished.

"Radio one ten-four," he attributed to his Boba Fet figure.

"Radio two here," Sailaja attributed to his Luke Skywalker figure.

"There's a bomb in my house!" he said.

"I'll call the police," he said. "Hello police?"

"That's us."

"We have a bomb at Boba Fet's house."

"Check, ten-four. We'll be there."

"Thank you! GOD bless America. Over and out."

"Boba Fet!"

"Boba Fet here."

"The police are on their way."

"Did you call the bomb squad?"

"No."

"Call the bomb squad!" he screeched.

"Hello! Hello! Bomb squad!"

"Yes, this is the bomb squad."

"We have a bomb at Boba Fet's house."

"Check! We're on our way."

"Roger, ten-four."

"Hello! Hello! Boba Fet!"

"Boba Fet here."

"The bomb squad's on the way."

"Ten-four." Sailaja got his C3PO and his Chewbacca figures in hand. He walked them over to Boba Fet and his Lego house.

"We are the bomb squad," Sailaja continued.

"The bomb's in here," said Bob Fet.

"You better stay out here while we go in," said C3PO.

"Okay." Sailaja put C3PO and Chewbacca in the house.

"Oh no! We're too late! It's gonna blow up! Run! Aaaah too late!" Sailaja then threw the house into the air and let it smash to the ground. C3PO and Chewbacca lay amongst the rubble.

"Aah, I'm on fire. I'm burning!" yelled Chewbacca.

"My legs are broken! I can't get up!" cried C3PO. Sailaja ripped off one of his legs. "Help!"

"I'll save you!" shouted Boba Fet. Sailaja pretended Boba Fet had a bucket of water. Splash! Splash!

"Thank you!" said Chewbacca.

"You're welcome." Then he moved over to C3PO and he grabbed his leg. "I'll fix you," Boba Fet then said. And he put C3PO's leg back onto his body.

"Thank you!" chimed C3PO.

"You're very welcome." Just then, Luke Skywalker pulled up in his Batman car.

He spoke, "I'll take you to the hospital."

"Thank you," choired C3PO and Chewbacca. Sailaja put them in the car and drove them off into the sunset.

"Sailaja!"

"Yes, Mama?"

"Time to go to the park. Come on downstairs." She grabbed his attention and he tromped on down. His Mother greeted him in the foyer. "Okay," she said, "shoes first. Give me your left foot." Sailaja put out his left foot. "Good!" she praised. "Okay, right foot." Sailaja put out his right foot.

"You are extremely intelligent," cooed his Mama. She velcroed him in and then they were ready. Out the door they went, Sailaja holding his Mother's hand.

"Maaama."

"Yes Sailaja?"

"Can we get ice cream?"

"Perhaps after we go to the park. Okay?"

"Yes, Maaama."

They arrived and walked onto the tot lot graveled area.

"Spin me on the merry-go-round, Maaama."

"Okay." They were at it within the minute. Around and around went Sailaja.

"Faster Mama! Faster!" His Mom spun him a little faster and he again called to go faster and so she spun him faster and faster. Sailaja laughed and laughed. There were other kids playing with their own parents. Ah, the childhood dance of jolly joy. Kids ran to and fro. Some played tag. Every one of them was having a great time!

Today is Thanksgiving. Sailaja's family goes to his Aunt and Uncle's house for dinner. They live in West Hartford, Connecticut. It is a long drive from their home in Virginia. They stay a few days. Sailaja sleeps on the floor in his sleeping bag. His folks get a spare bed.

"Sailaja!"

"Yes, Maaama?"

"Are you ready to go?"

"Yes, Maaama. Are you ready to go tooooo?"

"Yes I am, Bear. Maybe you should ask your Poppa if he too is ready to go."

"Okay, Maaama!" And Sailaja was down the hall in a second to get Poppa for the trip.

"Poppa!"

"Yes, Son?"

"Are you ready to go?"

"I'm ready if you're ready. Are you ready?"

"Yes, Poppa."

"Maybe you should ask your Mama and see if she's ready."

"I already did."

"Well then let's go, Little Monkey," said Poppa and then he screeched like a chimpanzee. Sailaja laughed.

I think we drove through California on our Thanksgiving trip. There was a big red horse on the side of the road with a sign when we went through California. I looked for California condors when we drove through California. The condors are extinct. I mean endangered.

I remember we drove through the mountains and it took us six or eight hours. Or was that the trip to Pittsburgh? I cannot remember which, but it was a long time. We ate tacos on the way. Mama and Poppa had coffee. I had hot chocolate.

When we drove through New York City, there were a lot of big buildings. I saw lots of big trucks on the highway too.

Here comes Aunt Debbie with the turkey. I'll eat some and so will Poppa, but Mama will not. She is a vegetarian. She eats asparagus and green beans. Oh, and bread.

"May we bless this meal," said Uncle Jack.

Uncle Kevin spoke, "Dear GOD, please bless all people on this and every day." No one said anything and then we all started eating and talking. It was a nice family day.

"I want some more turkey, Maaama."

"What's the magic word, Dear?"

"Please."

"Certainly, My little Man." And Mama got me more turkey. I ate light and dark meat. Mmmmm. It tasted good going into my belly. I ate a lot. Then I had to peep.

"Maaama!"

"Yes, Mashnoogeti?"

"May I be excused?"

"Are you done eating?" Mama asked me.

"I have to peep," I whispered.

"Okay," Mama whispered back. I fast-walked to the bathroom. Then I let it out. Luckily it was not a stinker. I went back in to eat.

My cousin Benjamin was already playing with cars. I wanted to eat more of the excellent food.

"Maaama..."

"Yes, Pumpkin?"

"Caaan I have more apple stuffing?" And there it was, more apple stuffing on my plate.

It is really a big process to prove everything is great, especially the holiday season of winter. Then I looked outside. I could not control my enthusiasm.

"Poppa it's snowing!" I exclaimed.

"It is! It is, Sailaja!" And then Poppa drank his whole beer, crushed the can and asked for another. "Dear, can I have another beer?"

"May I and yes, just a minute," and then Mama got Pops a beer.

"Thanks." Then we men watched the Steelers win the Turkeybowl. Mama was great, really great. Bless her soul!

Sailaja remembered his youth sporadically. Today was a good memory, but every day is better than the last so he has learned. To learn is not always easy. Back in time things were different. Ink and paper ruled, not the computer.

Christmas eve.

"Maaama!"

"Yes, Sweetheart?"

"Why do we have to wait until tomorrow to go and open the presents Mama?"

"Well dear, tradition I guess. It comes from even before Great Grandma's time. Yes, we've been opening gifts on Christmas morning since I was your age and so I pass this tradition on to you."

"But I want to open them now."

"Just like me, you'll have to wait until tomorrow."

"Poppa, I want to open them now."

"Listen to your Mother Son."

"Yes, Poppa. Oh, Poppa, why doesn't Jaleel have Christmas?"

"His family celebrates different holidays than ours."

"Oh." And Sailaja hung his head low. He was defeated. Times were tough, he thought. Sailaja had to be patient. He had to be brave. And all this while being a happy little boy.

"Maaama! Poppa!" Sailaja rallied. "It's snowing!" His parents awoke.

"Good morning, Butterfly!" sang his Mama.

“Merry Christmas, Sweet Pea!” called out his Poppa. Sailaja liked being called Sweet Pea just because. Sailaja jumped up onto their bed. He started jumping and singing.

“Jingle bells. Jingle bells. Jingle all the way. Oh what fun it is to ride in a one horse open sleigh. Hey!” Sailaja smiled bright as a light bulb.

“Are you ready to open your presents?” his Mama asked.

“Am I ever!”

“Well let’s go then,” his Poppa said as he climbed out of bed.

It was about a week later on New Year’s Eve.

“Maaama.”

“Yes, Sweetie?”

“What are you making Maaama?”

“Well, Dear, these are black eyed peas.”

“Black eyed peas?”

“Yes, Honey. It’s a tradition to eat black eyed peas on New Year’s day. It’s considered good luck. Up North some people eat sauerkraut on New Year’s Day for good luck.” Rain came down outside. You know the type of grey day where you do not want to go outside because it is cold and wet. A day where you turn the lights on inside and maybe read or do a puzzle, listen to music and tap your feet. Maybe a game. Yes.

“Maaama!”

"Yes, Sailaja?"

"Can we play 'Candyland'?"

"Let me finish what I'm doing and then we can play."

"What are you doing, Mama?"

"Adult things."

"But what is it, Mama?"

"Bills, Darling. I'm paying bills."

"Why, Mama?"

"Well, Dear, so we can have heat, and so we can drive our cars. It is how we keep our house…"

"Oh." His Mom finished up the bills by putting stamps on all the envelopes.

"Honey."

"Yes, Maaama?"

"Come on. We need to get your shoes on." And so they put on Sailaja's shoes.

"Where are we going, Maaama?"

"Out to the mailbox, Dear."

"Can I put the flag up? Can I put the flag up?" he asked twice with excitement.

"Certainly pumpkin." They each had an umbrella. It helped to keep their upper halves dry, but their feet got wet. Mama put the envelopes in the mailbox. Sailaja reached up and put the flag into position. He liked doing that and it made his Mom happy.

"Time for beddy-bye." Sailaja was already bathed and in his pajamas. His Mama got a book from the shelf. "Daddy, will you read to him tonight?"

"Sure, Mama. Come on, Monkey-man. Let's go to your room." Sailaja hopped up from his trucks and cars on the living room floor.

"I'm coming, Poppa." He got into bed in a jiffy.

Sleep.

It was lunchtime the next day.

"Do you remember this one Sailaja?" asked his Uncle Gerald who was visiting. His uncle was holding up his hand in the sign language position for 'I love you'. That is the pinky, the pointing finger, and the thumb extended with the two middle fingers down. Sailaja shook his head 'No'.

"It means I love you in sign language. That's how people who can't speak with their mouths speak. They use their hands." Then his Mama chimed in.

"We speak with our hands all the time when we wave 'Hi' or 'Goodbye'."

"Sometimes," Sailaja said, "we speak with our feet too."

"How do you mean?" asked Mama.

“Like this,” Sailaja responded. He lifted up his bare left foot and waved it back and forth. He let out a little chuckle, so did Mama and Uncle.

“We speak with our head too,” said Mama. “Ask me if I’m your Mama.”

“Are you my Mama?” he asked. She nodded ‘yes’.

“Ask me if I’m your Uncle,” said Mama.

“Are you my Uncle?” She shook her head ‘no’.

“Ask me if I’m the window.”

“Are yoooo the window?” Mama shook her head ‘no’. Now Sailaja caught the drift. He asked of his own accord. “Are you your hair?” Mama nodded ‘yes’. “Are you your water?” he went on. She shook her head ‘no’, then picked up her cup and finished the water.

“Now I’m the water,” she said. All three laughed.

“Say, Maaama?”

“Yes, Dear?”

“How come Daddy has to go to work so much?”

“That’s not something you need to worry about.”

“But, Maaama, I want to know.”

“Well, I guess he does it for money.”

“He gets money at work?”

"Not exactly, Dear. See, he works and from the company he does his work for, his company makes money and in turn they pay him money."

"Well I want him to work here."

"Well, Sweetie, I don't think that's possible."

"Why not?"

"He has to be at work so he can communicate with his co-workers. See they all work together."

"But why? I want Daddy here."

"I want him here too, but he has to go to work. See, without him working we wouldn't have food or clothes or even a place to live. That's what money buys us. That's why people work."

"But you don't go to work."

"Well Sailaja, I work to take care of you. To take care of this house. I do the shopping and the cleaning."

"Well then, since you work who pays you?"

"No one pays me. I don't work for money. I work as part of my duty to my family."

And so another day passed.

"Mama! Mama! Maaama!" Sailaja was downstairs and Mama was upstairs. Sailaja ran up the stairs.

"What, sweetheart?" Mama called to the ascending Sailaja. He got upstairs.

"Mama quick come down here with me."

"Okay, okay." She followed him downstairs to his bathroom.

"Mama, this is the fart room."

"Excuse me, Dear?"

"This is the fart room," Sailaja repeated and then he farted which was followed by a chuckle. His Mother did not know what to think. She did not know what to do. Then with little effort and GOD'S grace, she farted too. She laughed.

Today was going to be a long day. Sailaja and his Mama were at the garage for the state emissions test. At least one thing was right, Sesame Street was on the television in the waiting room. Sailaja loved Sesame Street. Television supervision passed time so simply. It seemed to take forever for the car to be ready. Sesame Street was long over and Sailaja became antsy.

"Maaama, when will it be ready?"

"Well, Dear, I don't know how long." Sailaja let out a sigh. His Mom knew what to do. She got a truck out from her purse and gave it to him. The waiting room became his play room.

"RRRRMMMM!" he let out as he rolled the truck up one side of the chair and "RRRRMMMM!" down the other side. He rolled that truck up and down the water cooler. Up and down the carpet. Up and down and all around that waiting room until finally…

"Ma'am, it's all ready." Mama took out her credit card. She paid. Then they were off to 'Children's Land', a combination toy store, restaurant, and indoor play center.

Sailaja loved it. They had a padded room full of balls for the kids to wallow through. There were tunnels and bridges, slides and swings. By the time they got home, Sailaja was berzerted.

As time went by, Sailaja *naturally* grew and soon it was his first day of school. For the first time in six years his Mama had the day to herself. Before she knew it, the mail was there. Realizing she had been sitting in the same chair for two hours, she got up and got the mail.

Meantime Sailaja enjoyed his new class. He played near the door. Mrs. Street, his teacher, mingled among her little people exemplifying her with-it-ness. All the kids were playing. Some fiddled with blocks. Others had cars and trucks. There were stuffed animals and 'Lincoln Logs'. Some pretended to read while others really did read. Crayons and color by number books. Blocks with letters and numbers on them. All in all, there was a lot of playing going on.

After a half day of meeting classmates and play, it was time for Sailaja to head home. Along with all the other parents, Sailaja's Mom appeared to take him home.

"Hi, Mama!" burst Sailaja. Later that night his Poppa came in to his room.

"Let me tell you something."

"Yes, Poppa?"

"Life is GOD'S big puzzle. You have to figure out which part you want to work on and get going. School can help with that."

"Yes, Poppa."

"Now go brush your teeth."

"Yes, Poppa." And Sailaja went to brush his teeth and then into bed.

This night seemed no different from any other. The sky was dark. The moon showed partially in the aura of clouds and stars. There was love in Sailaja's heart. He had done it. He had gone to school. It was not so scary, school and all. There were other kids his age or thereabouts. The teacher, she was so nice.

He went to bed. Little Sailaja drifted off to sleep, music now loud in his head. Dee da dee dada da dee dee. And how quickly he fell into the abyss.

That night he opened up his window and it was snowing, but he was not cold. He flew up into the descending snow. From a distance he saw himself in a black cloak, ascending to infinity. On this night he left the Earth behind and found another little person. A girl. Or a woman. It was tough to distinguish.

"Hi! My name is Emerald," she said and then giggled. She continued, "What's your name?"

"Sailaja."

"Sailaja, I've been expecting you."

"Where are we?" he asked.

"We are on the moon if you like," she said, but they were floating in a pitch black environment.

"If I like?"

"Or we can be in the park, if you like," she answered. He stared at her. She seemed to glow in blue and yellow mist. Not too bright, just hints here and there. And her eyes, they were big, wide, and yellow mixed with grey.

"Wake up Sailaja," he heard. The voice came from beyond and Emerald turned away. "Wake up, wake up. It's morning time," his Mama sang. "Wake up, wake up. It's breakfast time." Sailaja opened his eyes. The morning sun lit his room and there was Mama. Another day. He thought about Emerald, but said nothing of her to his parents.

Today, on his way to school, Dad said this, "My Mother once asked me what a mind was. The answer I told her two and a half years later, I said, 'The mind is the most amazing thing you can imagine.' And she simply said, 'Oh that's nice."

"Grandma?" probed Sailaja.

"Yes." Poppa looked over to Sailaja. Sailaja was looking at him too, the whole time. "Now Sailaja…"

"Yes, Poppa?"

"Remind me to stop at the thrift store for new clothes tomorrow."

"Okay, Poppa." And Poppa taught Sailaja in this way.

"MPFI son!"

"MPFI, Poppa," [Minimize Potential For Injury]. Poppa stopped his dull faded green 1972 FORD Torino and Sailaja went to school.

Two weeks later Sailaja found himself and his parents in Johnson City, Tennessee. They were in a burgundy four door sedan, a reasonable airport rental. It was a cold morning and the sky was a heavy grey.

Poppa rolled down his window. Three silver haired men in overcoats were standing there. Poppa spoke, "Jonathon Jaekes Jamilton Jaroo." The one man nodded and looked at his list.

"Yes, here you are. Please pull in behind that green truck." The truck was Sailaja's Uncle's. The night before was perhaps most chilling. They were in town because of Sailaja's Grandmother. She was, you see, now resting in the eternal sleep.

Poppa talked with various people while young pre-teen cousin Mary corralled Sailaja around the funeral home. It was close to eight in the evening when Poppa picked up Sailaja and walked over to the casket where Grandma lay.

Poppa spoke in a quiet voice. "Sailaja," he paused to find the words, "this is the last time we will see Grandma. Tomorrow we are going to bury her. She has gone to live closer to GOD and it is up to us to never forget her. Now close your eyes and ask GOD to bless her." Sailaja closed his eyes and spoke quietly aloud.

"Dear GOD, please bless my Grandma." Poppa silently prayed for a moment. He stood with Sailaja in his arms and walked over to where Mama was sitting. They all sat together as more family and friends came and went, mingled and left.

That night Sailaja, Mama, Poppa, and all of Poppa's brothers and sisters and their families went out to eat at Chez Gwompaire. There were many families. Kevin and Marian, Marian being Sailaja's favorite, and Tom and Sue, and Jackie and Raymond, big Raymond and little Raymond, Jen and Rachel and Rebekah, Grace, Carl and Patty, Ben and Tracy, Teresa and Jackson, Gerald and more. It was a big group. They talked over wine and pasta, gnocchi and bread, pizza and veal. It was a good time though the fact that one was missing loomed in the back of their heads, although these last few years Grandma stayed home during most of the large family outings. She was still missed on this night. In fact, she would be thought of for years to come when so much of her was such a big piece of the family pie.

Sailaja did not quite understand, but he saw the motionless body. He was told what had happened, yet he still played, running around ducking from cousin Mary at every corner. He did not realize the loss that all the older people realized. This night was just another night to him. It was the next day when the family of Jonathon Jaekes Jamilton Jaroo, Sailaja's Dad, pulled their rental into the auto processional line to follow the hearse from the funeral home to the church to Grassy Knoll Cemetery. They got out and walked inside. They were just in time as Father George began a group prayer. Every one repeated after him.

The funeral home guys closed the casket and the six pall bearers fell into place. They took the somber walk from A to B and put the coffin in the hearse. Everyone went to their cars and all lights were turned on.

They drove to the church where the six pall bearers escorted the coffin with Grandma inside. Everyone sat for prayer. In this church, a Catholic church, the ceremony is the same across the world, minus a few personal notes mentioned by the priest and family. After all was said and everyone took communion, they took Grandma in her coffin back out to the hearse and then into Grassy Knoll. Brief words at the site by Father George and all laid flowers on the coffin. They said goodbye. Some cried. Marian cried. The cold wind beat on Sailaja's exposed face. Just as they were leaving to go enjoy a meal in the church hall snow began to fall.

"Maaama! Maaama! Snow, Mama!"

"Yes Sailaja," she said eking out a smile as she wiped a tear from her cheek. Sailaja ate quickly and then it was back to cousin Mary corralling him around the room. There were many there, family and friends. All was respectable until three disreputable men entered the room. They removed their hats and long coats, hanging them with everyone else's by the front doors. They scanned the room and made eye contact with Poppa.

Poppa whispered in Mama's ear. The three men filled their plates from the buffet. They had ham sandwiches among other things. Pasta and stuffed cabbages. These three snakes slithered past other tables until they got to Sailaja's Poppa's table. They sat and one spoke.

"Jona [Jawnah], I know this is a tough time for you. We offer our condolences. We need to speak to you in private, perhaps when you are done eating."

"Okay, Neck." Now Poppa called him Neck as most who knew him did, short for Neck Breaker. It was twenty minutes later when Poppa approached Neck and his two associates.

"Okay Neck, what did you need to see me about?" asked Poppa.

"Well, it's about your Mother. I know she just passed and I would again like to offer my sympathy. She was a good woman."

"Yeah."

"Anyway, she owes us right near nine thousand dollars and since you're the oldest, I figured you to be the one to take a collection from your family. I know it is not a good time so I'll give you a couple of weeks to get it together." Poppa took a deep breath.

"Nine thousand huh?"

"To round it off, yes."

"Okay Neck. We'll get it together."

"I do appreciate your cooperation."

"Yeah, well we'll cover her debt." And that was that. Sailaja's Grandmother owed money to gangsters and for what Poppa would not even ask.

"I am ruler of the Ezkeeli Empire!" koomed Sailaja loud and powerfully. He was twenty five and acting in his first Broadway play. He was on the moon again with his old pal Emerald. She was with him everywhere. Oh, how he loved it. How it charged his brain and body for the most unholy acts of impropriety based on lascivious motivations. The stage floated everything into place with a standing ovation.

The play was a smash hit and being number one was a riot, but no, we must go back again. Back to the man who made it all possible. Sailaja owed everything to Tsalksuo.

"Everyone," said the teacher, "this is a new classmate of yours. His name is Tsalksuo." Just like that and there were now twenty one students in class including Sailaja.

“Hi. I’m Tsalksuo.”

“Hi to you too. I’m Sailaja.”

“I come from the Great Mother Earth,” proclaimed Tsalksuo.

“The Great Mother Earth?”

“Yes. We don’t eat animals. They are our friendly neighbors,” continued Tsalksuo.

“What do you mean you don’t eat animals?” queried Sailaja.

“That’s right! Just what I say. No animals.”

“Whaaaat? Are yoooou crazy?” asked Sailaja.

“No, I’m not crazy. I’m Tsalksuo and I don’t eat meat.”

“No chicken legs?”

“Nope.”

“No cheeseburgers?”

“Nope. And no hot dogs or fish either.”

“Whaaaat?” And so their day went on with Tsalksuo talking about his vegan lifestyle inherited from his father. He told how his sister ate animals following their mother’s example. At recess the kids made the teachers laugh while they engaged each other in their teacher conversations.

Hours later.

“Welcome home, Dad.”

“Thank you, Mom.”

“How was your day?” Mama asked Poppa.

"The new guy wouldn't stop talking about egalitarian pay scales."

"Sounds troublesome," Mama reflected.

"Yeah. Double trouble, Hon'."

"Well, Son, are you ready to go to sleep?"

"Suure Poppa!" Sailaja jumped in the air and kicked his legs out. They swooped off to Sailaja's room. On the shelves of his room there rested many gifts from friends and family. Pictures too. He had a wedding picture of his Mom's parents. A picture of her Grandfather, Jake, in his barber shop.

That night, Sailaja wondered why his new friend ate no animal products. He thought of the Sparzack's cat and the Scarborough's dog. He soon drifted off to sleep. In his dreams he remembered…

'The mind is the most amazing thing you can imagine!' The dreams went on and Sailaja enjoyed every moment of his sleep. In his dreams he could fly and swim under water without air.

This part of life we mostly forget.

Now Sailaja had school five days a week, just like the five days a week his father went to work. His new friend Tsalksuo had interesting lunches from home every day. Most curious was this thing called tofu, something his mother had eaten before.

"It's made from soy beans so it gives me all the right protein," Sailaja was told. With his tofu, he had different sauces, each uniquely aromatic. Spicy peanut sauce, sweet and sour sauce, plum sauce, and curry sauce to name a few. Tsalksuo also had fruits and vegetables every day along with spring water and juice.

"I am the most healthy kindergartener you'll ever meet," Tsalksuo told Sailaja. Sailaja wondered if that was true.

"Maaama?"

"Yes, Sailaja?"

"Tsalksuo says he is the most healthy kindergartener I'll ever meet. Is that true?"

"Well, Dear, that is a matter of opinion."

The very next day Sailaja told Tsalksuo, "You are not healthier than me. My Mama says that's just an opinion."

"You watch what you say to me!" whipped Tsalksuo.

"I can say what I want!" snapped Sailaja.

"I tell you now, don't speak to me!"

"You can't tell me what to do!" These two would have faced mediation, but they were at recess and out of the teacher's earshot.

"I'm warning you!" exclaimed Tsalksuo as he raised his fists into the air.

"You can't tell me what to do!" insisted Sailaja. Tsalksuo lunged forward and busted Sailaja right in the face.

"What you gonna do now?" yelled Tsalksuo. Sailaja burst into a wail and ran away to tell the teacher. By the time he got to the teacher he was crying and bleeding.

"What happened Sailaja?"

"Tsalksuo, uh, uh, uh hit, uh, uh, uh, me, uh, uh, uh."

"He did?"

"Uh, uh, uh, yeah, uh, uh, uh."

"Where is he? Can you show me?" Sailaja took the teacher to Tsalksuo.

"Tsalksuo."

"Yes teacher?"

"Sailaja says you hit him. Is this true?"

"No," Tsalksuo lied.

"No, huh?" asked the teacher.

"Yes you did! Uh, uh, uh…" cried Sailaja.

"Tsalksuo, are you telling the truth?" the teacher examined Sailaja as she asked Tsalksuo about his truthfulness.

"Yes," lied Tsalksuo again.

"Well can you explain why Sailaja is bleeding?"

"He fell off the tower," Tsalksuo quickly invented.

"Is this true Sailaja?"

"No. He hit me."

"Tsalksuo, why would Sailaja say you hit him?"

"Because I'm healthier than him."

"Tsalksuo, I think you need to apologize to him before we go to the clinic."

"No."

"Tsalksuo, please apologize."

"No!"

"Do we need to call your parents?"

"No! I didn't do anything!"

"Sailaja, you can go to the clinic now. Tsalksuo, I need you to come with me." Their teacher asked another teacher, Mrs. Morgan, to keep watch on her kids while she took Tsalksuo to the office. Tsalksuo did not return to class that day. That night Sailaja's parents discussed the incident at dinner.

First his Poppa complimented Mama. "Delicious dinner, Dear."

"Thank you, Sweetheart."

"Now Sailaja," Poppa articulated softly, "I understand another boy punched you in the face today. Is this true?" Poppa asked although he already knew it to be a fact.

"Yes, Poppa. It was Tsalksuo."

"I don't remember him," Poppa admitted.

"He is a new student," Mama informed him.

"Oh." Poppa continued, "Now do you know such behavior is inappropriate?"

"Inappropriate?"

"Yes, Son. Inappropriate. Not proper."

"Oh yes, Poppa."

"Well I suspect that boy is in trouble with his parents. Now Sailaja?"

"Yes, Poppa?"

"I hope you are not planning on fighting this boy again."

"No, Poppa."

"Okay, Son, good. Dear could you please pass the salad?" Another dinner was eaten and another night slept.

The very next day…

"Sailaja?"

"Yes Tsalksuo?"

"I'm sorry for hitting you. Can we be friends still?" asked Tsalksuo.

"Yoooou want to beeee myyyy friend?"

"Sure I do."

"Okay."

Time bounced by and soon Poppa was home from work.

"Poppa! Poppa! Guess what!"

"What, Little Man?"

"Tsalksuo apologized to me and asked to be my friend."

"Wow! What a good friend."

"Yeaeeuh!"

"Exciting news, isn't it, Mother?" Poppa said just before he broke out the flowers.

"It must be Friday. Poppa's got flowers," said Mama.

"It is, Maaama. It is Friday," interjected Sailaja.

"You know what else that means?" Mama asked the Little Guy.

"Fish dinner."

"And who gets to help cook?"

"I dooo!" Sailaja cheered.

Friday arrived and left, beginning another Saturday.

Sailaja went to sleep that night with a kiss from Mama and a noogy from Poppa. It took him a while to fall asleep. Quickly he dreamed.

"I am Gerousia [Jurroosha]!" came the voice in his dream. Gerousia was an ethereal presence without form or rationale behind it.

"Do not be afraid!" came a voice from beside him. Sailaja looked and standing beside him was Emerald, his dream friend.

"Hi Emerald," said Sailaja. Suddenly he could think and understand the world like his parents. Gerousia was the unknown. Emerald was his friend. Together, Gerousia and Emerald were here to teach him.

"Sailaja."

"Yes Emerald?" When Sailaja said this, he realized his voice was deep like his Poppa's. He looked at his hands and they were large and somewhat hairy. He knew he was dreaming, but this surprised him.

"When you go home, we have a mission for you," spoke the voice.

"What is it, this mission?"

"We, Gerousia and I, want you to remember," preened Emerald.

"Remember what?"

"Just remember."

"Sailaja!" came Mama's voice. "Wake up! Wake up sleepyhead," she sang. "Get up, get up, get outta bed! There be no sob sobbin' when the red red robin comes bop bop bobbin' along! Sweet song!." Sailaja awoke. 'Remember', he thought.

"Good morning, Maaama."

"Good morning, Dear."

"Mama?"

"Yes, Dear?"

"Can I have pancakes for breakfast?"

"I think I can arrange that."

"And Mama?"

"Yes, Pumpkin?"

"Can I have maple syrup too?"

"Sure, Sweetie."

That night Poppa watched the news.

"Environment! Environment! Environment! I cannot stress it enough," said the anchor. Then Mama walked into the room after putting Sailaja to sleep. She sat next to Poppa.

"Do you know what a spokeswoman on TV said a few minutes ago while you were with the Bean?"

"Tell me Poppa."

"When a woman has a baby, then the government should give her a gift of money as a seed for their child's university or vocational education."

"Sounds impossible, but it would be nice."

"Imagine it, Honey, free money from the government."

"It's kind of like a tax break, but made to sound different than that."

"That's right."

Sailaja was in school the very next morning.

"Mrs. Street, I don't feel too good," said Sailaja.

"What's wrong, Dear?"

"My stomach hurts."

"Do you need to go to the nurse?"

"Uh huh," replied Sailaja as he nodded in affirmation.

"Okay, Mrs. Park," she said, "I'm going to walk Sailaja to the clinic. I'll be back straight away."

"Okay." And they walked to the clinic, but they did not make it there in time.

"Hooouh!" came the noise as Sailaja vomited onto the floor. 'Oh dear!' Mrs. Street thought.

"Try and hold it in, Sweetie, until we can get you to the nurse." But it was no use.

"Hooouh!" came the noise again as Sailaja bent over, splashing the hallway carpet.

"Oh Dear!" Mrs. Street said out loud.

"Hooouh!" came the puke again. And so the hall began to smell like breakfast and stomach acid. Moments later they arrived at the clinic. Sailaja was in bad shape. The nurse called his home on the telephone.

"Hallo," answered Mama.

"Hi, this is the nurse at Terraset Elementary."

"Yes."

"Sailaja is in with me. He is pretty sick and we are hoping you can come to pick him up."

"My car is in the shop. I will have to call my husband."

"Okay, the sooner the better."

"What is wrong with him?"

"He is hacking and has a fever."

"Poor baby! We will be in for him right away."

"Okay." Forty five minutes later Poppa arrived at the school. Sailaja was sweating and had a bucket by his head where he lay.

"Hey little King," Dad soothed. "I'm gonna take you home." Sailaja looked at him, but he said nothing. He did not even give Poppa the usual smile. The ride home was unpleasant for Sailaja. He had nothing left in his stomach to spew. He had the dry heaves. Poor Little Guy. Mama greeted them at the door. She touched Sailaja on the head as Dad carried him into the house. They took him directly to his bed. That was where he spent the next twenty four hours. Fever and cold sweats. The doctor said to give it a day before bringing him in. Chicken broth did not stay down at first, but late that night it did. He dozed on and off in exhaustion. By the next afternoon he was totally asleep in dreams.

There came his friend and the voice of Gerousia.

"Listen to Gerousia," Emerald beseeched.

"Sailaja, you must try to remember," and with this the light of the setting sun through his window awoke him. Remember what? He wondered. His sickness had left him. He slid into his slippers and went to the living room where Mama and Poppa were reading.

"Hi, Sweetie," cooed Mama.

"How ya feelin' Son?"

"Good."

"How about some french toast?"

"Yeah, but can I have it with maple syrup and sliced strawberries?"

"Oh course, Darling."

That night…

"Politics, politics. I think sometimes that is all work is about."

"Give me an example, Husband."

"The other day, Dave said he'd been married three times and has nine children. Then George said he was married twice and has five children. Then Kenneth said he's only been married once but has seven children. Then I thought, but didn't say, I've been married six years next week and we have one son. I took my tea and went back to my office."

"How's that politics, Dear?" asked Mama.

"I guess I see it that way because in other places around the globe, and yes, even in America, people are permitted to have more than one spouse. I mean religion shouldn't be included in State affairs, yet it is illegal for practitioners of many religions to follow their established customs of marriage, and so at work we talk about our gripes. I can't say exactly what we talk about, but it just seems like politics when we do."

"Okay."

"My office has," continued Poppa gruffly, "eight foot windows on one side. I have a computer and an four hundred dollar chair. My position controls other folks." Poppa realized how he had raised his voice. "I'm sorry, Mama. I didn't mean to raise my voice at you." Mama was looking at Poppa wide eyed. He said more, "And I don't know what to think about all these troop deployments and war whoopin'."

"Hopefully we'll be able to resolve it all through diplomacy," reflected Mama.

"Hopefully," Dad agreed.

"Goodnight, Poppa."

"Goodnight, Son."

"Goodnight, Mama."

"Goodnight, Sailaja."

"Thanks for the story."

"Anytime, Monkey." Soon after the light was turned out, Sailaja began to float and he looked at his arms and they were adult sized and so were his shoes and yes, all of him was adult. Sleep. Artworks flashed by him. Posters of bands he collected like Gorilla Biscuits, Flex Your Head, Soulside, and Bad Brains. More important images of Jesus and Dr. Martin Luther King Jr. and Gandhi and Nixon. Sleep.

When Sailaja awoke he rolled from bed. He immediately realized he was not in the bed he went to sleep in. In fact it was a different room. When he looked at the bed there was a woman sleeping. Then he noticed his hands and his feet were not small. There was writing on his toes, tattoos he somehow knew. The tattoo said 'LOVE MY GIRL'. What was going on?

"Good morning, Sail," said the woman.

After much confusion, Sail found himself at a desk in an office building wearing a tan suit and a blue shirt. Tan tie. He put his feet up and listened to the traffic outside. What had he missed? There was a gold band on his left ring finger. Married. On his desk was a picture of his wife, the woman from his bed. He got to thinking. Where did all the time go?

Then it got deeper. He had a picture of his wife, sure enough, but no kids. That night he got home. Sail tingled with excitement.

"So when do you want to start having kids?" Sail asked. She smiled. She thought he would never ask.

"Are you serious?" she asked.

"Totally, Dear!"

"But you always said we should not have kids."

"I did?"

"Yes, every time we talk about it."

"Well I've changed." He went on, "We can start tonight. You can get off the pill." She was overjoyed and had always hoped for this day.

"What do you want first, a boy or a girl?" she asked.

"Let's just hope it's healthy."

"I can live with that," she replied. His wife hugged him big and gave him a wallop of a kiss. It was on!

The next day Sail awoke and he looked in his mirror to see white hair. As he found his way about the house, he saw pictures of children now so familiar to him. He finally sat down and began writing his first book.

It was not a book of autobiographical nature, nor of academic consequence. The book he started was a book of poetry. Some rhyming. Some free verse without rhymes. In a year he had one hundred and three poems. The day he finished he went to sleep early. His kissed his wife goodnight. As sleep crept upon him, a familiar face appeared.

"Hi Sail," she said. "Do you remember me?"

He did.

"Are you Emerald?" Sail asked.

"Yes my friend. Are you ready to come with me?"

"Come where?" he asked.

"Into the land of dreams."

"But what of my sweet wife and all my kin?"

"All in time. You have finished your book so now we can go."

"Will I not be able to say goodbye?"

"That is what your book is for." Suddenly Sail saw he was in a lush garden with all sorts of plants and fruit trees.

"May I have an apple?" he asked.

"Of course, Sail."

"I have always wondered if my memory of you was true. Now it appears to be so."

"This hour I am known to you. Am I not the same friend of childhood dreams? Am I not the most beautiful woman you have ever seen?"

"I am afraid to answer that," Sail hesitated, "for fear you shall curse me."

"Be honest. You have none to be scared of now. We dwell with the angels."

"Well then, you are not the most beautiful woman I have ever seen. My wife is. She and then my Mother and my Daughters and my Grand Daughters. Will you now let me return?"

"I am sorry, but that is neither here nor there any longer. Look into your mind and you shall see them as they do you. Hear their voices as you think they can of you." Sail thought and there they were, sitting in their great room by the fire. He was still not with them which made his heart ache. He wished they could touch him and he touch them. Emerald spoke.

"Shall we fly a while?" she asked.

"Fly?" he questioned.

"Yes, if you wish." Sail noticed he felt light and looked down. He was floating. Emerald was now floating too. "Just think it," she said.

Sail slowly began to rise and he felt new. Fresh. Emerald followed and they both rose nearly a hundred meters into the sky. They were not yet in the clouds when an eagle soared by in the close distance. The Sun shown clear and warmed Sail.

"Glorious!" he exalted.

"Yes! I agree," replied Emerald. "Do you still wish to return?"

"Return where?" asked Sail with confusion.

"To your home. To be with your family." This struck Sail, for moments ago he had wanted to return, but now he was engulfed with this defiance of science.

"Can I think about it? Do I have time?" he asked.

"As much time as you want." And so they spent about an hour soaring with the birds. Indeed this was the most fun Sail could remember.

They soon returned to the ground where they collected various fruits and vegetables for a meal. Sail wanted to cook potatoes, but had no matches or a lighter and no pot or pan.

"How shall we start a fire?" Sail wondered out loud.

"Think it," replied Emerald.

"Think it?"

"Yes."

And Sail put some sticks in a pile, looked at them and thought, 'Fire'. The sticks instantly caught fire. He was as amazed with this as with flying, though so completely in the present that his amazement slipped away.

The meal was ready, but they had no plates. Then Sail saw Emerald use a large leaf to plate her food. Sail got up and picked a large leaf from a lettuce plant. He joined Emerald for hot potatoes and steaming squash as well as apples, bananas, and oranges.

After eating they laid back in the grass and dozed off for some rest. When Sail awoke, Emerald was cuddled up to his back. This startled him for he had not slept with another woman, other than his wife and kin, in over fifty years. However startled he was, it indeed felt good and he lay awake until she stirred and awoke.

"Hi," she said with a yawn.

"Hi Emerald," he returned.

"Are you ready?" she asked.

"Ready for what?"

"Just ready."

"I guess."

"Close your eyes and think of something," she said. Sail did and he thought of riding on an elephant. "Okay," she said. "Open your eyes." He opened his eyes and there before him stood an enormous elephant, more enormous than he realized it would be.

"Ready for a ride?" Emerald asked.

"I've never ridden on an elephant and for the record, never seen one except on TV."

"Well now's your chance." Momentarily he was mounted on the beast.

"How do I get him to walk?"

"Still learning I see," she replied. "Eeuh!" cried Emerald and the elephant began to walk. She walked beside them.

'I wonder what will happen next?' thought Sail. After ten minutes, Sail dismounted and the elephant sauntered off into the distance. Just before the bull elephant was out of sight it trumpeted, celebrating his freedom.

Emerald took Sail's hand and all of a sudden swarms of butterflies descended upon them. Blue and black and yellow and orange. Quite astonishing! Sail had never seen so many butterflies. Emerald smiled at Sail and then asked him to look to the sky. There were two rainbows with not a cloud in sight. They were there. It was amazing. Yes.

With a closing and an opening of Sail's eyes, he and Emerald were on a ferry at sunset, riding toward the Statue of Liberty. There were other people around yet Sail felt as if upon a pedestal with Emerald, shining in the crowd.

It is now that Sail realized he was no longer an old man, nor a young boy, but an ageless man of youthful skin and tiger-like physique. Momentarily, Sail and Emerald were hovering about the head and face of the statue. Then they were in a field of cut grass with a picnic feast before them.

"Wine?" Emerald asked.

"Red please." She poured some into a silver goblet for him to savor along with the sushi and steak tartar. Had life ever been this enticing? He wondered. Soon after the meal they dozed off with Emerald curled up to Sail's back. Spooning. She put her arm around him just before falling asleep.

Mmmm.

Sleep!

The dwelling of dreams. Surreal where we meet those passed, awaking and recalling the joy of interacting with one or another we thought gone forever. He felt Emerald put her arm around him.

Thank you, GOD, he thought. After a rest, how long they did not know, Sail and Emerald awoke and had sushi with the blink of an eye. Next they took a walk by gorgeous waterfalls and had a fresh drink from a spring. Then they ate lamb, skinned that day, lamb so tender, with carefully prepared mouth-watering garlic and onion mashed potatoes. They ate.

"What shall we do now?" said Emerald.

"Scrabble!" Sail smiled saying this. "With a party of all my family who have passed away and those I have never known."

And so this becomes their future, meeting those long gone who have been celebrating ever since they passed.

Sail and Emerald were at some sort of party. His Pap Pap grabbed him, between dances with Bettie, and they had shots of whiskey and a cigarette while Bettie and Emerald discussed the children (Pap Pap and Bettie were his grandparents who had long since passed away). They had more shots. Pap Pap pulled him close as an unfamiliar man entered the party. "That's Jim, my brother!" Pap Pap smiled wide, eyes wild. "Wait 'til you meet him!" exclaimed Pap Pap and then he danced away with Bettie, big band wailing away!

Jim approached. "May I sit with you?" he asked.

"Certainly," Sail said.

"I'm Jim," he said with a grin, "and you are Sail. I've been waiting for you."

"How did you know who I am?"

"Let's just say I've got connections. Scrabble?" And so Jim, Emerald, and Sail had a game of Scrabble which they finished off with shots of the good stuff. Jim got the best word of the game, XYLOPHONE, which he got by adding XYLO- as a prefix to –PHONE and incidentally, also got the triple word score.

"Pure luck!" Jim exclaimed.

"Looks like we got us a ringer, Emerald." She agreed as all three laughed. Sail was overjoyed to be meeting Pap Pap's Brother.

"I've been watching over you my boy," Jim told Sail.

"Really?"

"That's right!" Jim said proudly. "You wouldn't believe how many times I saved your life. Do you remember that time when you were seventeen at that party where that dude tried to brain you with a baseball bat?"

"Oh yeah. Yeah!"

"Well, I used my majigga to stop him."

"Thank you."

"No thanks required. Or that time your wheel fell off on the north south highway?"

"That was you?"

"Yeah. I kept you from going into oncoming traffic."

"Now that was a scary!"

"A couple other times too."

"I've always thought there was someone or something watching over me."

"Well, you were right," said Jim with a chuckle. And he looked about the party, catching an unfamiliar eye. "Would ya look at her!" And then Jim was up. "Excuse me," he said and he went straight to her, a beautiful woman. Sail nor Emerald had ever seen her before.

"Want to dance?" asked Emerald.

"I don't really know how," said Sail.

"Still learning?"

"Oh, my fault." In a moment they were dancing up and down the floor, jigging with happiness. After hours of meeting new relatives and getting reacquainted with those known before, Sail grew tired. He and Emerald decided to have a rest in a heart shaped hot tub and then sleep on a futon in front of a blazing hearth. The sleep was deep. Sail dreamt about his children. They played outside in their above-ground pool. They were splashing and laughing. Even their dog jumped in for a moment.

Then Sail woke. Emerald was curled up to his back. It felt good. He wondered if what they had was love. In the very next instant, he chided himself for being unfaithful. But was this the afterlife and if so, was he free to make new passion? Before he decided, Emerald awoke.

"Good morning," she said. "Sleep well?"

"Yes."

"Anything you'd like to talk about?"

"No," said Sail defensively, secretly. For now at least, he thought he would keep his confusion to himself.

"What would you like to do?" she asked.

"Learn all that is and that ever will be." Emerald smiled devilishly. "What?" Sail asked.

"Still learning, huh?"

"What do you mean?"

"You still don't know, do you?" she asserted.

"Know what?"

"The essence of all and all you need to do."

"No I don't. Would you tell me?"

"Try closing your eyes and asking our CREATOR." And so Sail closed his eyes and nothing came. He opened his eyes.

"Nothing," he said.

"And what did you expect to find?"

"I don't know. Maybe Heaven or Valhalla or Nirvana. Things unknown that when known would be familiar."

"What am I?" Emerald asked. Sail had not thought much about it. He had just been flowing with the moment and not analyzing. Now he did.

"You're an angel," he purported.

"Guess again."

"If you're not an angel then you must be some sort of heavenly creature."

"To tell the truth," she said, "I cannot define myself. All I can tell you is that I am here for you."

"For me?"

"That's right."

"What for?"

"For whatever you want." Sex came into Sail's mind and he felt himself blush. He wanted to say, 'Let's get naked!' His next immediate thought was that she is a woman, and as such, sacred. Emerald was a thing to be cherished and held dear. She was not some piece of meat to have hedonistically for supper.

"Sex!" she exclaimed.

"No," he assured her, "not sex." Then she reached out and ran her fingers up his bare arm.

"What about my wife?" he asked.

"She isn't here."

"But I wouldn't feel right."

"How about now?" she asked as her garments disappeared. Emerald looked ravishing. Sail looked away.

"You can look now. My clothes are back on." He looked again and she was wearing her clothes. "You can't forget her?" Emerald posed.

"No. She was my only love, even more than my kids and my grandchildren," Sail replied.

"What about me?"

"What about you?"

"Can't I offer you anything?"

"You have, yes."

"Does that not merit some favoritism?"

"You are different, though. You are magic."

"Tragic more like it."

"No," Sail said, "fantastic is more like it."

"Then why don't you want me?"

"Do you mean sexually?"

"In one aspect, yes."

"Well, Emerald, when you were naked I felt like I was breaking a law. A vow."

"You mean like one of the Ten Commandments?"

"Yes, but also my personal vow to GOD to be faithful to my wife until death."

"What if I said you were dead? What if I told you there are many people who believe in having many wives?"

"I just see my wife in my mind on our wedding day, our promise to be true."

"I see," said Emerald. "Perhaps we should consult Gerousia. Do you remember Gerousia?" inquired Emerald.

"The name lights a candle, but no, not really." Suddenly everything went pitch black. Then the two were illuminated without any particular light source.

"Oh Gerousia!" Emerald called, "We need your guidance." No answer. Soon he fell asleep. It was a glorious sleep, unlike any ever before. While Emerald and Gerousia spoke, Sail slept.

"I think he is worthy," Emerald decreed.

"No one is worthy. Who is this human?"

"You met him years ago."

"Of course. Ah yes, the bad kid."

"Yes, the bad kid," confirmed Emerald.

"Not worthy!"

"Do you remember the thing he did that he can't remember doing?"

"That's why he's called a bad kid."

"Yes, I remember now," said Gerousia, " and only a couple of fist fights as a young one. Nothing else violent, but he..." Gerousia stopped talking and put his gaze upon Sail.

"He was a Father. A Grandfather. A Great-Grandfather, before we rejuvenated him."

"Perhaps he is ready for the final test," decided Gerousia. Emerald said nothing, but looked intently at Gerousia and then the Gerousian presence was gone.

The choice was Sail's to make. This was a matter between many forces, but most important, it was a matter of FAITH. GOD.

"GOD," said Sail to himself. "I made a vow to YOU and to my wife. This is a serious decision. What should I do?" GOD smiled. Sailaja knew what he had to do.

"Emerald," he said, "I will not break my wedding vow."

"And so it shall be," Emerald proclaimed. Sail had proven worthy.

It was time to wake up.

"Remember," Emerald said.

"Sailaja! Sailaja!" called a distant voice. Sailaja was dreaming about his friends whom he had lost during his life. Emerald was gone. "Sailaja!" called the voice.

"Sailaja!" came the voice again. He finally stirred. For a moment he remembered everything and then he woke up. There was his Mama. "How would you like chocolate chip pancakes for breakfast?" Sailaja was a little boy again.

"Okay, Mama! Can I have orange juice and bananas and maple syrup too?" he asked.

"Whatever you want, Angel."

"Mama?"

"Yes, Dear?"

"I was skateboarding in my dream."

"What else were you doing?"

"I think I was supposed to remember something, but I forget," Sailaja answered.

"All in good time my dear. All in good time," his Mama said. And so Sailaja was granted a second childhood with all the hopes and dreams humanity has for him. It turns out, this time around, Sailaja would be a good kid. Sailaja's Mama went out and raised their flag. It was another glorious day!

It was years later in his teens when he proved to be better than he had before. It was in the streets of Richmond, Sail saw a guy he knew to be affiliated with an organized white power racist group. Sail knew he had to act.

"Hey!" Sail yelled as he burst into anger. "Ain't you one of them Nazis?"

"That's right!" sneered the racist bastard.

"May we speak seriously for a moment?" Sail asked as he approached.

"Okay."

"Do you realize that we are in a world of unrest?"

"Yes." The racist agreed.

"Do you understand that you hating others prejudicially adds to such unrest?"

"Understand that I'll teach you a lesson if you don't shut your mouth."

"Okay." Sail then turned and walked away. He had planted a seed of thought in the guy's mind and so he began his career as a forester of the mind. This is quite a worthy occupation, beginning life where there was only potential, planting seeds.

So Sail moved along in life trying to do good. He did well in school and tried to make his parents proud.

They were.

It was a balmy summer day years later, just right for swimming at the beach. He and three friends hopped on the highway and arrived at Virginia Beach just in time to miss the worst of the sun. The girls in bikinis were everywhere.

She wore pink.

He wore black trunks.

Pink and black. They locked eyes. Sail walked over.

"Hi," he said. "My name is Sail."

"Hi," she said. "I'm Mary Jane."

"*Mucho gusto*," he replied. "That means pleased to meet you in Spanish."

"Oh. *Mucho gusto* to you too."

"Where are you from?"

"Here. How 'bout you?"

"I'm inland. Richmond."

"Oh." She smiled.

"You wanna get something to drink?"

"Sure," she said. Sail was so excited. As a man of forestry, he thought now was as good a time as any to continue in his career. He would plant another seed.

He said this as they drank their cold lemonade, "If you marry me, I promise to always be true to you and do my best to listen to you. To care for you and to try to make you happy." Mary Jane laughed, more like giggled.

"Who says I want to marry you? We just met," she then said.

"I just wanted to let you know. You wanna know a secret?"

"Okay."

"If you marry me, I'll tell you." He laughed and so did she.

Then she said, "Are you always this entertaining?"

"Never," he said with a smile. And so Sail would join with Mary Jane and live happily ever after.

Afterward

Once as a little boy I closed my eyes and opened them to a different world. Not a safe place, but one of danger and oppression. Where there had been love, peace, and safety, it all vanished. Terror appeared at this juncture. Reality that our world is ruled by the gun became apparent all in one moment. One blink. Life became a trial through which I made my way. It was all I could do to be positive, yet negativity surrounded me. Enveloped by hate and violence, our planet seemed doomed. There were people killing others over material objects.

A car. Shoes. Drugs. Fuel. It all came down to borders and money. The with and the without. As I grew into a young adult, the subtleties of beauty snuck into all the pain and suffering. A tree's leaf or the satisfaction of a glass of water. Sail jumped through all this with ease as he moved through his days into surreality and back to the world where science makes sense.

My life is much longer than Sail's as are most human lives. To find the pleasing aspects of our lives we must look with blinders and have faith in a greater being who causes all to ebb and flow.

War, famine and disease ravage parts of the world while we in the United States of America sell weapons internationally. We stockpile food and make essential medicines unavailable to our poorer neighbors. Is the answer Christianity and compassion?

No.

Compassion yes, and parts of Christianity as well as other Faiths. We need altruism to bring necessities to all of our world neighbors. Sure compassion, but compassion without ethnocentrism. Ethnocentrism basically means thinking there is one correct way to do things and that your way is how others should act. Acceptance of others without trying to Americanize everyone.

Some might say the answer is anarchy and peace combined. If so then who shall build our roads and bust monopolies? Who then would fight thuggism and jail psychotic murderers? I can see the appeal of peace, but not with anarchy attached. But how?

We need to end the billions wasted on fighting drugs and re-invest in education and technology. Does it really make sense to make war on a country's own population? And we need to define more reasonable prices, making healthcare universally affordable. It may be time to heal rather than compete. We need to remember how it feels to lose. It does not feel positive. Today millions starve, live in fear of Corona Virus, or are not free to voice opinions. Even in our nation, the United States, peaceful protestors are jailed, maced, or shot with rubber bullets. No wonder riots erupt. There is widespread dissatisfaction with how our leaders and other leaders across the globe tell untruths and live double-standards for themselves, the elite.

It is time to call on all virtuous leaders to hold value for all peoples. Only this will allow humanity to heal and forgive.

In the fictitious story told in this book, Sail simply bounces through his existence. In our World everything is more complex. Take this to heart. Accept that we all must do our part to bring unity and understanding to all corners of the Earth. If we forgo these roles then we should not once complain of our individual plights and be satisfied with inequality which may one day bring those who are complacent to their knees, begging for the mercy of the infinite ALMIGHTY.

I find myself stuck overnight in Chicago's O'Hare airport. Realizing I have to wait until the morning flight, seven hours away, calmness overwhelms me. It is chilly here outside, but quite warm inside. Winter. There is no snow. This book will soon be typed- soon means within a year. My sister-in-law says I seem collected. Here's to you!

No worries. No hurries. For now this story is over. I will draw.

If you think then I offer you gratitude. If you do not think then now you must. In prayer solutions are found. Some call prayer meditation. With effective communication solutions are achieved. Some put GOD aside or say there is no GOD. Understand. All achievement is under GOD.

Made in the USA
Middletown, DE
16 November 2024

64708337R00124